Neen reached out to trace the pattern on her teacup. "Why does this project mean so much to you?"

Rico blew out a breath. "As soon as the café is up and running and I have the figures to prove its success, I can start canvassing for funds for additional cafés in other parts of the city."

"You want to run a chain of charity cafés?"

"Why not?"

She couldn't think of a single reason. Except... "Don't you ever stop for fun?"

He didn't answer that.

The Redemption of Rico D'Angelo

Michelle Douglas

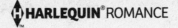
HARLEQUIN® ROMANCE

Recycling programs
for this product may
not exist in your area.

ISBN-13: 978-0-373-74262-2

THE REDEMPTION OF RICO D'ANGELO

First North American Publication 2013

Copyright © 2013 by Michelle Douglas

Printed in U.S.A.

At the age of eight, **Michelle Douglas** was asked what she wanted to be when she grew up. She answered, "A writer." Years later she read an article about romance writing and thought, *Ooh, that'll be fun*. She was right. When she's not writing she can usually be found with her nose buried in a book. She recently completed an English master's program for the sole purpose of indulging her reading and writing habits further. She lives in a leafy suburb of Newcastle, on Australia's east coast, with her own romantic hero—husband Greg, who is the inspiration behind all her happy endings.

Michelle would love you to visit her at her website, www.michelle-douglas.com.

Books by Michelle Douglas

THE CATTLEMAN'S READY-MADE FAMILY*
FIRST COMES BABY...**
THE LONER'S GUARDED HEART
THE NANNY WHO SAVED CHRISTMAS
BELLA'S IMPOSSIBLE BOSS
THE MAN WHO SAW HER BEAUTY
THE SECRETARY'S SECRET
CHRISTMAS AT CANDLEBARK FARM
THE CATTLEMAN, THE BABY AND ME

*Part of the *Bellaroo Creek* trilogy
**Mothers in a Million* series

Other titles by Michelle Douglas available in ebook format.

To my wonderful niece, Abbey,
who loves books as much as I do.

CHAPTER ONE

RICO STARED AT the application in front of him—again—before blowing out a breath and slumping in his chair. He'd had such high hopes for this project—hopes of finding someone as fantastically enthusiastic about it as he was.

His lips twisted. Hopes of finding someone not only fantastically enthusiastic but with first-rate qualifications and solid experience to bring to the table as well. A day and a half into the interviews, however, and he'd found he could kiss that notion goodbye.

He straightened. Punching a button on his intercom, he barked, 'Is Janeen Cuthbert here yet, Lisle?'

'Not yet, but there's still ten minutes until her appointment.'

'Thanks.'

Wasn't it an unspoken rule to arrive ten minutes early for a job interview? He scowled at the wall opposite. Restaurant managers, it seemed, worked to their own schedules. Not that Hobart's restaurant managers were beating a path to his door for the opportunity to run a charity café.

He slammed Janeen Cuthbert's file shut.

Pressing thumb and forefinger to the bridge of his nose, he tried to breathe through the pounding at his temples, tried to push it back and concentrate. He'd thought he'd be able to find *one* community-inspired restaurant manager with a few street smarts in this rotten city.

He wasn't greedy. He only wanted the one. How hard could that be?

He'd had community-inspired people, all right. He'd had sunny, bright and earnest applicants without a scrap of experience between them. Nice people. But he could see the likely outcome all too vividly. The boys would walk all over them, would dishearten and disillusion them. There'd be tears and tantrums. And then they'd be gone, leaving him in the lurch. This project was too important to risk that.

He glanced at his watch. Five minutes to two. If Janeen Cuthbert wasn't here at two on the dot then she could just turn around again and march straight back home. She might at least have worked in a café, but he needed someone who would take this job seriously. He needed someone fully committed to making this café work.

For the next five minutes he drummed his fingers against his desk. He didn't turn to look out of his window at the busy Hobart thoroughfare below. His wasn't one of the offices that afforded a glimpse of the harbour. As he was rarely in his office, however, he didn't much care. As a project manager, he didn't even have his own secretary. He had to share Lisle with two other governmental project officers. He didn't much care about that either. He'd long since come to the conclusion that if you wanted a job done, you did it yourself.

He glanced at his watch. Two p.m.

He went to push the button on the intercom, but Lisle beat him to it. 'Janeen Cuthbert is here for her two o'clock appointment, Rico.'

He gritted his teeth and swallowed. 'Send her in.'

He counted to three. A soft knock sounded on his door. He swore under his breath. That knock was too soft. It was the kind of knock that lacked backbone. His hands fisted. Darn it! He'd had enough of sweet and nice and inefficient to last him a lifetime.

He tried to uncurl his lip. 'Come in.'

When he clapped eyes on his penultimate interviewee, however, he immediately reassessed his prior judgement. Ms Cuthbert didn't look as if she lacked a backbone. In fact, she looked boiling mad, as if she were about to explode. She hid it well, but he'd spent too many hours working with troubled youths not to recognise the signs—the glitter in her eyes, the colour high on her cheekbones and the flared nostrils. Even if it *was* all tucked away beneath a polite smile.

He stared at her and his shoulders unhitched a fraction. She might be a lot of things, but he was suddenly certain the one thing she wasn't was meek and mild.

'Mr D'Angelo?'

He kicked himself forward from behind his desk. 'Yes.'

'Pleased to meet you. I'm Neen Cuthbert.'

She strode across to him, hand extended. It was bright red, as if it had recently been scrubbed to within an inch of its life. He briefly clasped it and then stepped back. She wasn't wearing pantyhose and her knees were bright red too.

It wasn't her hands or her knees that held his attention, though. Her dove-grey suit sported four equidistant pawprints—two on her thighs and two just above her breasts. No amount of scrubbing could hide those. For the first time in two days he found himself biting back a smile.

When his gaze returned to her face, her chin went up a notch, as if daring him to say one word about those pawprints.

'I'm pleased to meet you, Neen.' He kept his voice even and some of the glitter eased from her eyes. He pursed his lips and then shook his head. 'I suspect your afternoon has been as stressful as mine.'

A flash of humour lit up her face. 'It's that obvious, huh?' She glanced down at the pawprints, her lips twisting. 'It has been something of a trial,' she allowed.

'Please, take a seat.' He motioned to a chair. Moving back around his desk, he stabbed a finger to his intercom. 'I know it's going above and beyond, Lisle, but could we possibly have coffee in here?'

'Coming right up,' she shot back cheerfully.

To his mind, the other two project managers took thorough advantage of their shared secretary. Rico didn't see coffee making as part of Lisle's duties. In this instance, though, he was prepared to make an exception.

'That was kind of you.' Neen's glance was direct. 'Truly, though, you didn't have to do that on my account.'

He waved that away. 'You may not thank me once you've tasted it.' It wouldn't be café standard by any means. 'But, to be perfectly frank, I could do with a hit of caffeine.'

'I take it your interviews aren't going well?'

He stiffened at her question, realising how unprofessional he must appear. He shifted on his chair, fighting a frown. He'd let his guard down. He couldn't remember the last time that had happened.

He shook his head. He needed a holiday.

He shook it again. He didn't have time for a holiday.

'It's hardly surprising, though, is it?' she said, obviously misinterpreting the shaking of his head. 'You want a highly qualified and experienced restaurant manager, but the wage you're offering is hardly attractive.'

'And yet you applied.'

She pointed to her file on his desk. 'As you'll have

no doubt ascertained from my résumé, I'm not what you'd call highly experienced.'

'And yet you *still* applied?'

'And you decided to interview me.'

Okay, she definitely had backbone. She might not be cheerful and earnest, but she definitely had backbone, and that trumped cheerful and earnest any day. At least for this particular job.

Lisle came in with two steaming coffees. After she'd left he asked, 'What happened?' He gestured to the pawprints.

He made it a vague gesture, because he didn't want her to think he was checking out her chest. He hadn't been going to ask, but her criticism of the wage he was offering made him dispense with the niceties. Besides, he held those pawprints entirely responsible for his momentary lapse. If he found the answer to their mystery, he could then concentrate on getting this interview, and himself, firmly back on track.

She'd started to lift her mug, but at his words she set it back down with a thump. She didn't spill a single drop, though. 'Nothing today is going as planned. I came in here prepared with a pretty speech about why I'm the best applicant for your job. Instead I make snarky comments about the remuneration package and…'

Just for a moment her shoulders sagged. In the next instant, however, she straightened them again.

Her eyes suddenly danced and she seized her coffee and sipped it.

'I mean to enjoy this,' she raised her mug in his direction, 'because I'm guessing it doesn't much matter what I say from here on. And after the day I've had I'm not going to beat myself up about it.'

She was mistaken if she thought she was out of the running. Not that he had any intention of telling her so. Yet. 'Well?' He raised an eyebrow.

She cradled her mug in her hands and crossed her legs. One of those red knees peeped out at him. 'My flaky neighbour has landed me with her dog—gifted him to me, would you believe?—while she jets off to Italy for some indefinite amount of time on multiple modelling contracts.'

He gestured. Again, vaguely. 'So the dog...?'

'Montgomery.'

'Did that?'

'He did a whole lot more than that. You should see the state of my navy suit and my pantyhose.'

She lifted the mug to her lips and took a sip. He watched, fascinated, as she closed her eyes in what he guessed was bliss. He reached for his own mug and took a sip too. It was good. He let out a breath he hadn't even been aware of holding. The tightness in his shoulders eased a fraction more.

'It's hardly Monty's fault, though. Audra's never trained him, and at fourteen months he's not much more than a puppy still.'

He stared at those pawprints. 'What kind of puppy?'

'A Great Dane.' She shook her head in disgust. 'No pretty little Chihuahua or toy poodle for Audra. Oh, no. She thought that a cliché. She wanted to be the model with the Great Dane. She thought the photo opportunities would be fabulous.'

'But?'

She suddenly grinned. It changed her entire bearing. Backbone: tick. Sense of humour: tick. Whoever won the position would need both of those in spades.

'Oh, the photo opportunities were there, but unfortunately they weren't to Audra's advantage.'

A chuckle broke free from his throat. The images Neen's quick sketch evoked were alive in his mind. 'Why did you agree to take him?'

'Ah, well, that would be because she snuck him into my apartment while I was in the shower, left a note explaining it all and then hightailed it for the airport.'

The act of someone who knew Neen couldn't be taken advantage of. 'What are you going to do with Monty?'

He shifted on his chair. Would she call the pound? He could hardly blame her. But...

'I guess I'll have to find a home for him.' She sent him a smile of such extraordinary sweetness it momentarily stole his breath. 'Mr D'Angelo,' she purred. 'You look exactly like a man in need of a dog.'

He stared. He floundered. Finally common sense reasserted itself. 'I'm not home often enough. It wouldn't be fair to the dog.' Inside him, a grin built. The minx!

All of her sweetness vanished. 'If only everyone who decided to get a dog had half as much foresight,' she muttered, and the grin inside him grew. 'There should be some kind of dog-ownership test that people have to pass before they're allowed to get a dog.'

'The same could be said for having kids.'

She stared at him for a moment. 'Your troubled youth, huh?'

'Disadvantaged,' he corrected.

'Semantics,' she shot back.

'I'm not saying they don't have issues. But all they need is a chance.' Which was where he came in. 'The purpose of the café is to train underprivileged youths in basic waiting and kitchen-hand skills, with a view to finding them permanent employment in the hospitality industry.'

She drained her mug, set it on the desk and then leaned towards him, her eyes suddenly earnest. 'Mr D'Angelo, I wish you every luck in your endeavour. I also thank you for the brief respite and the coffee.'

'Neen, you're not out of the running.'

She'd started to rise, but at his words she fell back into her chair. She gaped at him. 'I'm not?'

'No.'

Her eyes suddenly narrowed. 'Why not?'

He laughed. It was sudden and sharp and took him completely by surprise. But…a healthy dose of suspicion wouldn't go astray in the job either, and

Neen was ticking all his boxes. 'Not all the applicants have been a total waste of time,' he assured her. 'There's a couple who have potential.'

'But?'

'I'm questioning their commitment.'

She sat back and folded her arms. 'Why aren't you questioning mine?'

He didn't even need to think about it. 'You're honest, and I need that in an employee. You also have grit and a sense of humour, and I suspect both of those traits will be necessary in this particular job.'

She unfolded her arms. 'So you're not going to sugarcoat the position and tell me it's the job of a lifetime?'

'It'll be a challenge, but a rewarding one.'

'Hmm.' She didn't look convinced on that last point.

'And you're a dog-lover.' That made a difference. Dog-lovers generally got on well with kids, and—

'No, I'm not.'

He blinked.

'I loathe dogs. I can't stand them. They're noisy, smelly, stupid creatures. I'd much rather have a cat.'

It was his turn to gape. 'But you're still trying to find Monty a home. You haven't given him up to the pound.'

'It's not the dumb dog's fault his owner has abandoned him.'

He leaned towards her. 'That means, then, Neen Cuthbert, that you're a person of integrity. And that definitely ticks my boxes.' The day suddenly seemed much *much* brighter.

'What about my lack of experience?'

Her lack of experience *was* an issue, but... He pulled her résumé towards him. 'You've been working in the hospitality industry in one shape or another since you finished high school eight years ago.'

She nodded. 'I've been a waitress, a short-order cook, and I've worked for two big-name catering firms.'

None of her positions, however, had carried the title of restaurant manager. 'I see you recently completed a small business course?'

'My long-term goal is to open my own café.'

'That's ambitious.'

'I think one should dream big, don't you?'

He did.

'What do you think you can bring to the advertised role, Neen?'

Her eyes danced again. 'Besides honesty, grit, a sense of humour and integrity, you mean?'

She was right. He opened his mouth. With a superhuman effort he snapped it shut again. He still had one more applicant to interview. And he wasn't given to impulsive gestures or decisions.

She sobered. 'I'll work hard, Mr D'Angelo. That's what I have to offer you.'

The way she said it made it sound like the most valuable thing in the world. And it occurred to him that perhaps it was.

'I've been acting manager on numerous occasions at most of the establishments I've worked for, but it has never been part of my job description. I want the experience your job will provide me. In return for that I will work hard. And I won't let you down.'

He believed her. There was just one final question. No, two. 'Why are you currently unemployed?'

She hesitated. 'There are personal reasons.'

He leaned back and waited to see if she would tell him.

She stared at him as if assessing him, as if weighing whether he needed to know the truth and if she could trust him with it. Eventually she lifted one shoulder. 'Earlier in the year I was left an inheritance. I planned to put the dream of my own café into action at once.' She smoothed her hair back behind her ears. 'The will, however, is being contested.'

She didn't need to tell him what a blow that had been. He could see that all too clearly. 'I'm sorry.'

She lifted her chin. Her cool blue eyes were veiled. 'These things happen. Until it's sorted out it seemed wise to find another job.'

She obviously wasn't the kind to sit back and wring her hands. He had the distinct impression that, like him, in times of stress she liked to keep busy.

He picked up his pen and tapped it against her file. 'One final question. Would you be prepared to sign a two-year contract?'

'No.' She spoke without hesitation.

The weight slammed back to his shoulders. The day went dank and grey.

'I would be prepared to sign a twelve-month contract.'

It was something, he supposed. But it wasn't enough. It was a shame, because on every other point Neen Cuthbert had been perfect.

The next morning Rico sifted through his shortlist of three applicants. He rang the nominated referees for his first two choices.

He discounted the most experienced after speaking to the man's former employer. 'Talented pastry chef with five years' worth of managerial experience' did not make up for 'hot-headed and temperamental'. Hot-headed and temperamental were the last things this project needed. He needed a manager who would create a nurturing environment.

Nurturing and no-nonsense. Which immediately brought Neen Cuthbert to mind.

He thrust her out again and checked the references for his other shortlisted candidate. They were impeccable.

On impulse he seized Neen's file and rang her referees too. Their testimonials were glowing. If he didn't give her the job they'd take her back in an instant. *'I want the experience.'*

Rico chewed the end of his pen. He paced the length of his office. This job was too important for him not to get it right. He strode back to his desk and set Neen and the other applicant's résumés side by side. Neen's rival had a fraction more experience, but…

Why on earth was he dithering? Helen Clarkson was prepared to sign a two-year contract. *Commitment!*

He swept the applications up and shoved them back into his folder, then strode out into the outer office. 'Lisle, can you phone Helen Clarkson and offer her the position? If she accepts she'll—'

'I just got off the phone to Helen. She's accepted a position in Launceston.'

She'd *what*? What about all her talk of commitment?

Lies. All lies!

Neen hadn't lied.

'Fine!' he snapped. 'Offer the position to Neen Cuthbert. Tell her she'll need to come in and sign the contract one day this week.'

'Roger, Rico.'

He slammed back into his office. He had a mountain of paperwork to get through and grant acquittals to write. Not to mention grant applications. Securing funding for his projects was an ongoing challenge and not something with which he could afford to fall behind.

An hour later he threw down his pen. Too much of this bureaucratic red tape always set his teeth on edge. He strode to the door and flung it open. 'Did you get onto Neen Cuthbert?' he barked at Lisle.

'She was delighted to accept.'

'Excellent.' He glanced at his watch. 'She lives in Bellerive, doesn't she?'

Lisle flicked through her files. He could have told her not to bother—he'd practically memorised Neen's file down to the last detail.

Lisle held up the file. 'Yes, she does.'

He took it. 'I have a lunch appointment with the manager of Eastlands Shopping Centre.' He was trying to convince the man—so far unsuccessfully—to sponsor a programme to provide traineeships for unemployed youth in the area. 'While I'm on that side of the harbour I'll drop the contract off to Ms Cuthbert.'

Lisle handed him a copy of the contract without a word. She'd grown accustomed to his bull-in-a-china-shop approach long ago. 'You know Harley's job is going to be advertised next week, don't you? You should think about applying, Rico.'

'I'm more use on the ground, Lisle.'

'You're wasting your talents.'

'I'm happy where I am.'

He was making a difference. A real difference. And happiness didn't come into it.

'Oh, for pity's sake, Monty, give it a rest,' Neen muttered under her breath. She reached over and ramped up the volume on the radio in the hope of drowning out the dog's great booming bark.

She'd get complaints from the neighbours if this kept up, but…

Her hand tightened around the red pepper she'd started to dice. She just needed half an hour to get the worst of tonight's dinner prepared and then she'd let him back inside. Without her full attention he'd wreck her apartment. Knowing she was inside, however, he was obviously intent on barking…and barking…and barking until she did.

She knew he was lonely. She knew he missed Audra. She knew he simply craved some company. Poor dumb dog. If he could be trusted just to sit at her feet and chew a bone…

She glanced around at her chewed-to-within-an-inch-of-its-life furniture and shook her head. She opened the kitchen window instead. It looked out over the courtyard. 'Hey, Monty!'

He came charging up. Barking, barking, barking.

'If you keep up with that kind of nonsense,' she chided, 'how will you ever hear what I have to say?'

He quietened for a moment. The radio blared. She dragged in a breath. For good or ill, she had a way with dogs. 'What we need to work out is the kind of home that would be best for you. Do you have any thoughts on the subject? I'm thinking no small children, as you'll only knock them down, and—'

He started barking his head off again. She continued to slice the onions, cabbage and red peppers for this evening's stir-fry.

'What I was thinking was a lovely big property

where you could run about to your heart's content, and…'

He didn't stop barking. He no longer looked at her, just barked and barked. Her chopping slowed. She glanced at him again. In fact, he seemed to be barking at a point behind her and—

Her nape prickled. In the reflection of the window, something moved.

Whirling around, she held the knife out in front of her, every muscle tensed and readied.

A broad male figure loomed in the kitchen doorway. Adrenaline flooded her. Her heart clawed up into her throat. She gripped the knife harder.

The figure raised his hands very slowly in a gesture of non-aggression and then he backed all the way down the hallway and out of her house until he stood on the other side of her screen door. Only then did her pounding brain recognise who it was that stood on the other side. Rico D'Angelo. Her new boss.

Her heart didn't stop hammering. Her hands didn't unclench.

Rico raised a hand and knocked. She didn't hear it. Undoing her fist enough to reach out, she turned off the radio. 'Quiet, Monty!'

Amazingly, the animal obeyed her.

'Neen, I'm sorry I frightened you.'

She suddenly realised she was still holding the knife. With burning eyes she threw it into the sink. She gripped her hands together at her waist and tried to stop their shaking, tried to swallow the lump lodged in her throat. The lump dislodged itself to settle in her chest.

'Mr D'Angelo.' The shaking wouldn't stop. 'I… uh…come in.'

He shook his head. 'I don't think that's a good idea. I just wanted to drop this off.' He held up a sheaf of papers.

Monty promptly started barking again and her head throbbed in time with each booming sound. God, how to explain? She pressed her shaking fingers to her temples.

'How about a walk? I take it that's Monty, there? It sounds as if he could do with one.'

Gradually, little by little, her heart rate started to slow. 'I'm sure you're busy.'

'I dropped by so we could discuss a few things and to get your signature on the contract.'

The normality of their conversation after her over-the-top reaction finally returned her pulse to normal.

'I know I should've rung first, but I had an appointment in the area so I thought I'd drop by on the off-chance you'd be home.'

She needed to get out of the house. She needed to find a sense of equilibrium again. 'If you're sure you have the time?'

'I have the time.'

'I'll just get Monty's leash.'

She clipped the lead to Monty's collar, led him through the house and locked her front door. She averted her gaze from the carport opposite and her car, with its four slashed tyres. She hoped her enigmatic employer hadn't noticed them. She bit back an oath, her hand tightening on Monty's lead. Mr D'Angelo must think he'd employed an utter fruitcake!

'I'm pleased you accepted the position of café manager, Neen. I have great hopes for the café and I know you're the perfect person to head this up.'

His smile was too kind, too compassionate…too knowing. His tone too well modulated. She bit back a sigh. 'You saw the tyres, didn't you?'

Monty chose that moment to try and yank her arm out of its socket. Without a word, Rico reached across and took the lead from her. He smelled of cold air and peppermint.

'It happened today?'

She folded her arms and nodded. 'Which begs the question, why was I so careless as to leave the front door unlocked, doesn't it?'

'Monty?'

She bit back a sigh. 'It was all I could do to stay on my feet when I returned from the supermarket. Monty is always so…so delighted to see me.' She could have sworn that she'd locked the screen door, but she mustn't have. *So foolish.*

She closed her eyes and hauled in a breath. Ever since she'd received the news that Grandad's will was being contested, her head had been in turmoil. Not to mention her heart. Her concentration was shot to pieces. It had to stop! She had to start paying attention again. *She had to.*

'Have you reported the incident to the police?'

'Yes.' She swallowed and risked glancing up at him. 'Mr D'Angelo, I'm very sorry for…um…' Her stomach churned. What if she had stabbed him? 'I'm a bit jumpy at the moment.'

She made him stop when they reached the end of the block.

'Monty, sit.' The dog stared up at her with his big dopey eyes. She made a hand signal. 'Sit.' He continued to stare at her. She folded her arms and looked away. Eventually he sat. 'Good boy.'

She fondled his ears and then nodded to Rico. They set off across the road and then turned right towards the park and Bellerive beach.

'He's improving,' she murmured, more for something to say than anything else.

'Look, Neen, I'm the one who should apologise. I shouldn't have come in like I did and I'm sorry I startled you.'

His eyes were dark, almost black. She didn't doubt his sincerity for a moment.

'I knocked and knocked, and I could see you at the end of the hallway. I called out…'

'But between Monty and the radio—' and her own too-busy thoughts '—I couldn't hear you. It's not your fault, Mr D'Angelo. You don't need to apologise.'

'Rico,' he ordered.

The name suited him in one respect, with his dark Italian good looks, but Rico sounded breezy and carefree. She wasn't sure she'd ever meet anyone *less* carefree in her life. He was a man on a mission—an important mission. And, like most do-gooding types with a quest to save the world, he carried that world around on his shoulders.

They might be broad shoulders, but nobody could carry around that kind of weight forever.

He suddenly stopped and swung to her. Monty strained on the lead. It could pull her completely off balance, but it barely seemed to register with Rico.

'Look, I couldn't help noticing that yours were the only tyres slashed. Is something up, Neen? Is there something I ought to know?'

A weight pressed down on her chest when she realised she'd have to tell him—in the interests of his staff's safety. It grew heavier when it occurred to her that in their interests he might in fact retract his job offer.

For a moment she could hardly speak. The sun that glinted off the expanse of water in front of them dimmed. Finally she gestured to the remaining distance between them and the beach. 'Let's go down there and let Monty tire himself out.'

When they reached the sand Rico's hand hovered uncertainly on the lead's catch. 'Are you sure he won't run away?'

No, but… 'He'll stay on the beach,' she promised. She'd learned that much.

Without further ado he released Monty and the giant dog charged helter-skelter straight into the water, spraying it in all directions.

Rico shook his head. 'You're going to have sand everywhere when you get home.'

'Sand is something I can vacuum up. And it's preferable to him chewing the furniture. An hour of this and he'll be a relative lamb for the rest of the afternoon.'

He turned to her, hands on hips. She shrugged. There didn't seem much point in delaying the inevitable conversation.

'The slashed tyres aren't an isolated incident. The police are aware of the situation but there's not much they can do.' She pulled in a breath. 'Four months ago I broke up with a man who, it appears, can't take no for an answer.'

'And he's persecuting you? Threatening you?'

She lifted one shoulder. 'I have no proof that to-day's tyres are his handiwork.' But she knew in her gut it was. 'I've taken a restraining order out on him.'

And she *still* couldn't believe she'd left her front door unlocked!

CHAPTER TWO

'Neen?'

Rico touched her arm and Neen started. He immediately backed up, his eyes darkening. She wanted to reach out and tell him it wasn't him, but...

But what? Was she going to let Chris turn her into a timid mouse? Was she going to let his behaviour rule her life?

She leaned across and clasped Rico's arm. 'I'm sorry. I was a million miles away.'

Beneath the crisp cotton of his business shirt, his arm was firm and warm, vibrant, and her fingers were curiously reluctant to release him. For a few precious seconds the solid feel of him reminded her there was more in this world than her worries and troubles.

And while she continued to focus so closely on her troubles she was missing out on a lot of those other things—on laughter and friendship and... and simply being young. She'd applied to manage Rico's café hoping it would provide her with some much-needed distraction. Eventually Chris would get bored and give up. She crossed her fingers.

In the meantime she would not sit around and spin her wheels while she waited to see what the outcome of Grandad's will would be. She'd get experience, she'd become even better at her job and…

She swallowed. And she wouldn't focus on her sense of betrayal. That was what.

Rico watched her through narrowed eyes that saw too much. She tried to find a smile. 'It's been a while since there's been an…incident. I've obviously become careless.' She frowned. 'But…'

'But?'

In the spring sunshine his hair gleamed dark, but she could pick out the deep auburn highlights that threaded through it. While he'd shrugged out of his business jacket, his tie was still perfectly knotted at his throat. She shoved her hands into her pockets to stop herself from reaching out and loosening it.

'Let's walk for a bit,' she suggested, because standing there staring at him seemed suddenly absurd. Besides, the sand was packed tight from the outgoing tide. He shouldn't get too much sand in his beautifully polished leather shoes.

He fell into step beside her. 'What were you going to say?'

She shrugged, trying to replay that moment when she'd returned home from the supermarket. She'd unlocked the door…Monty had barrelled into her… she'd pulled the screen door shut so he couldn't escape and…

'It's just that I'm pretty certain I *did* lock the

screen door.' It was an action that had become second nature.

'How certain?'

'Ninety per cent.'

A second passed. Rico's hands clenched. 'You think someone picked the lock?'

Her mouth dried. 'I'm probably being paranoid, that's all.' She pressed her hands together and prayed that was all it was. 'About a week after Chris and I broke up I came home after work one night to find my entire apartment open—front door, back door and every single window. He must've still had a key. That was the first time I moved. The second time was after I woke one morning to find the house I'd rented splattered with red paint. I don't want to run like that again.'

She would *not* be turned into a fugitive.

Rico's right hand formed a hard, tight fist. She stared at it for a moment before glancing back out at the water.

'I have deadbolts on all the doors and windows, but not the screen door. Normally I don't leave the doors open, but it was so lovely and sunny today, and I…' For heaven's sake—it had been the middle of the day and broad daylight!

'You should be able to leave your front door open without fear of reprisals.'

He spoke fiercely and a lump lodged in her throat. She closed her eyes, counted to three and then shoved her shoulders back before turning to face him.

'I have been distracted today, though. I was offered the job.' She flashed him a smile that was meant to reassure him, but it didn't seem to do the trick. 'And I have a dinner this evening that I'm really stressing about. I need it to go well.' If it didn't… Her gut clenched. 'It's why I banished Monty to the courtyard. I just needed thirty minutes to get the dinner preparations sorted. I was trying to work quickly and I was focused on chopping and quietening the dumb dog.'

'And after the slashing of the tyres you were understandably jumpy.'

He didn't make reference to her over-the-top reaction. He didn't have to. It hung in the silence between them. But for several terrified seconds this afternoon she'd thought she'd have to fight for her life. Her mouth dried all over again at the memory. She hadn't realised how spooked she'd become.

She clenched her hands. She would not allow Chris to do this to her. She might not be able to control his actions, but she could control her own. She had no intention of letting her guard down again, but she'd allowed her life to shrink. That had to stop.

There was just one last thing…

'The incidents had become fewer and fewer. I thought perhaps Chris had finally given up. And, honestly, it's illegal for him to come within twenty metres of me. The moment he does I can throw the book at him, and I doubt very much he'd risk that. However, as he obviously hasn't given up would you prefer it if I stood down as your café manager?'

He halted and planted his hands on his hips. 'Why would I do that?'

She didn't say anything, just let him come to the same conclusion she had.

He frowned. 'You think he might start targeting your place of work?'

'I don't pretend to know what goes through his mind. It's a possibility, though, isn't it?'

'I'm not letting some sociopathic freak of a bully determine who I will or won't employ!'

Just for a moment she glimpsed something in him beyond the self-possessed, preoccupied executive. Something dark and dangerous that should have had her backing away but actually had her wanting to edge closer.

'I know you're the right person for this job.'

She stared at him, at the fire in his eyes, and the weight of his expectation slammed down on her shoulders, making them sag.

'But for heaven's sake, Neen, what possessed you to go out with a jerk like that in the first place?'

She hugged her arms about her waist and started walking blindly up the beach again. She'd been searching for love. She'd ached for it. That was why she'd fallen for Chris. He'd focused all his attention on her in a way nobody in her life had before— except for Grandad—and she'd lapped it up like a starving woman. Like the stupid, weak woman that she was.

It was only later that his possessiveness and jealousy had come to light. Or at least that she'd recognised them for what they were. If she hadn't been so needy she might have realised sooner and she could have ended the relationship then. But she hadn't, and now she was paying the price.

'I made a mistake,' she said when she was sure of her voice. 'Haven't you ever made a mistake?'

She glanced up, but his face had frozen into a dark mask.

He gave one hard nod and a curt, 'Yes,' and then swung on his heel and set off back the way they'd come.

She glanced around—Monty was still splashing in the water beside them—and then dashed to catch up with Rico. 'I'm sorry. I didn't mean to make that about you.'

He blinked and the mask disappeared. 'I'm the one who's sorry. It's hit me what a high price innocent mistakes can carry. It hardly seems fair.'

She took in the knotted tie, the polished shoes, and wondered what mistakes lurked in his past.

'Take the youth I work with. Most of them are paying for other people's mistakes. It's not their fault they were born to teenage mothers or have parents who've turned to alcohol or drugs.'

'And you want to make a difference?'

His eyes flashed. 'I *will* make a difference!'

For some reason his words chilled her. Or perhaps it was the tone in which they were uttered.

'Have you ever taken self-defence classes, Neen?'

It wasn't a question designed to dispel the chill that gripped her. She chafed her arms. 'No.'

'Why on earth not?' He reached out and pulled her to a stop. He dropped his hand again almost immediately. 'Surely that's one of the sensible precautions you can take?'

She turned away from him and stared out across the water and up at Mount Wellington, which towered over the city of Hobart, dominating it.

'Neen?'

She finally turned back. 'I kept hoping I wouldn't need to, that the threat wouldn't become physical.' She scanned the beach and the park beyond. 'Besides, I suspect he's watching me, following me. I haven't wanted to give him any ideas.'

Rico stared down at Neen and his heart clenched. She seemed suddenly small and fragile. His hands fisted at the thought of anyone hurting her—at the thought of any man hurting a woman.

Knowing how to protect herself against a physical assault was vital, even if it wasn't a fact she wanted to face. He didn't know if her ex—this Chris—would actually resort to violence, but it would be better for her to be prepared.

Besides, knowing she could physically handle herself would empower her.

He straightened and readied himself for an argument. 'Self-defence classes have just become a mandatory requirement for the position you were offered this morning, Neen. It's one of the things I came around to discuss with you.'

Her jaw dropped. 'Ooh, Rico D'Angelo, that's a big, fat lie.'

For a moment he thought she might even laugh. He'd like to see her laugh. He frowned and dragged his attention back to the matter at hand. 'It was an oversight of mine that I forgot to mention it when I interviewed you. The fact is you'll be working with disadvantaged youths. Some of those kids have been brought up by the scruffs of their necks.'

'And violence is a language they know?'

'Fluently.'

He had no intention of staffing the café with anyone who had that kind of a question mark hanging over them, but... He stared at Neen and his blood ran cold. 'I don't think we'll run into those kinds of problems, but you will be dealing with teenagers.'

'And teenagers can be hormonal and unpredictable?'

He let out a breath when he realised she wasn't going to put up a fight. 'So can some of their parents and friends. It's the world they've grown up in.'

'Which you're trying to change?'

He read the scepticism in her eyes. He should be immune to such scepticism—he fought it every working day of his life—but for some reason hers burned and chafed him. He rolled his shoulders and tried to dismiss it.

'The café budget will cover the cost of your self-defence classes.' She looked as if she was about to argue and he held up a hand. 'I insist. I'll be the one choosing the trainer, and I'll be receiving reports on your progress too.'

She blinked.

He'd make sure he chose the best. He couldn't believe this hadn't occurred to him before. If he could get more funding for future initiatives of the same nature, he'd make it an essential requirement for all his managers.

'I'll wait to receive the details from you, then.'

She turned to survey Monty and he couldn't help noticing how the sun picked out the lighter strands in her chestnut hair. 'I can't believe how much energy that dog has.'

Monty still frolicked in the waves—chasing them as they receded, snapping at them and leaping over them as they rolled in. The dog's utter physical joy in being alive struck him.

He shook himself. What was he thinking? He was too busy these days for swimming and beach-combing. He set his jaw. And he didn't regret it. Not one bit.

He swung back to Neen. 'In the meantime...'

She raised an eyebrow.

He'd make sure her class started asap—next week if he could arrange it—but... 'It won't hurt for you to

have a couple of pointers now. Remember, if someone does attack you, your primary goal is to disable
them long enough to get away. You don't want to
stick around and fight someone who's bigger and
more experienced than you are.'

'Right.'

He set her square on to him. 'If your attacker
comes at you from the front, like this—' he made
as if to grab her shoulders '—I want you to knock
his arms away like this, then grab a fistful of his
shirt and knee him in the groin as hard as you can.'

She eyed him doubtfully. 'As hard as I can?'

'Believe me, any jerk who tries to grab you de-
serves everything you can throw at him.'

'Right.'

'And scream. Scream your head off as hard and
as long as you can.'

Nine times out of ten fear of discovery would
have an assailant hightailing it for the hills. 'Now
turn around.'

She did.

'If an attacker grabs you from behind, like this—'
he seized her around the shoulders, pulling her hard
back against him and pinning her arms to her sides
'—I want you to—'

He broke off as a growling, snarling dog hurtled
towards them. Monty had been transformed from
boisterous goof to frightening assassin in a blink,
and Rico watched in frozen fascination.

Neen, however, was caught by no such abstraction. Before he had the wit to push her behind him she'd reefed out of his hold and boomed, *'No!'* at Monty, holding one hand straight out in front of her like a traffic cop.

The dog skidded to a halt, kicking up sand.

'Down!' she commanded in a hard, loud voice, making a demanding downward motion with her hand.

Monty whined and pawed at the sand.

'Down!' She repeated the hand signal.

Monty lowered himself to the ground, resting his nose on his front paws, but his eyes remained glued to Neen.

'Dogs work on a system of hierarchy,' she told him in a much softer, more modulated voice.

'Uh-huh.' His heart-rate started to slow.

'I need Monty to know that you're higher in the food chain than he is, so he learns to treat you with respect.'

He swallowed. 'Happy to help out in any way I can.'

'Shake my hand.'

He did.

'Now keep hold of it and bend down so I can kiss your cheek.'

He did as she bade and her scent hit him hard— a mixture of strawberries and oakwood…and dog. Cool lips touched his cheek and something in his chest lurched. Suddenly every bad-boy impulse he'd spent the last ten years repressing roared into ear-splitting life.

And then she moved away, although she kept hold of his hand. It gave him a chance to drag a steadying breath into his lungs. It was the beach. It had to be. All this sun and sand. It had been a long time since he'd stopped to enjoy either. And being here felt like a holiday.

'Monty.' She kept her voice soft and clicked her fingers. The dog immediately rose to nuzzle her hand. 'Put your hand down to him, Rico, so he can smell it, remember it…and apologise.'

Rico did as she said, not the least afraid Monty would bite him now. Neen's confidence had filtered into him, and he knew she wasn't the kind of woman who would put anyone at risk. Monty promptly licked Rico's hand.

'Good dog,' Neen said, finally releasing Rico and giving Monty a lusty scratch all the way down his back.

The dog groaned and arched against her. Rico didn't blame him one little bit.

'How come you know so much about dogs?' he asked, in an attempt to take his mind off the curve of her hips in those jeans that she wore. *The sun. The beach.*

'I grew up with them.'

'But you don't like them.'

'That's right.'

He watched as she pulled a tennis ball from her

pocket. 'Okay, Monty, let's really wear you out.' And she threw it.

Rico shook his head. 'My teenagers aren't going to know what's hit them.'

Neen returned home from the beach with Monty early the next morning to find workmen waiting by her front door. Her palms turned clammy. She scanned the complex and its surrounds, but nothing looked out of place.

Except for the workmen. Her hand tightened about Monty's lead as she approached them.

'Are you Ms Cuthbert?' one of them asked. At her nod he said, 'We've been booked to fit new screen doors, as well as security systems to each of the five apartments here.'

She straightened. 'Who hired you?'

He glanced at his clipboard. 'The real-estate agency responsible for these properties.' He named the company.

'May I see?'

He handed the order form across to her. As he'd said, the agency's name appeared in the requisite box, but she didn't doubt for a single moment that Rico was behind this somehow. Exactly how escaped her, but she was starting to see he was the kind of man who got things done.

'I'm Unit Three.' She handed back the order form. 'Shouldn't you start at Unit One?'

'The tenant in Unit One is away, and the real-estate agent isn't available to open the place up to us until tomorrow. According to my records Unit Two is currently vacant so, again, we have to wait on the agent.'

Audra's apartment. Or at least it had been.

'If you have any enquiries I've been told to direct you to the real-estate agency. Do you mind if we start work now? It should only take us an hour... two at tops.'

'Not at all.' She had no intention of looking such a gift horse in the mouth. She unlocked her front door and gestured inside. 'Be my guest.'

She sat in the courtyard with a pot of tea while Monty dozed in the patchy spring sunlight. On impulse she pulled out her phone and punched in the number Rico had given her.

'D'Angelo,' a voice barked without preamble, and for some reason she found herself having to fight back a smile.

'Hello, Rico, it's Neen here.'

'Is everything okay?'

'Yes, thank you.'

It was a long time since anyone had made her feel so cared for.

Her hand tightened about the phone. Wanting to be looked after, taken care of, loved, was what had got her into this trouble in the first place.

'I...um...I just wanted to thank you. I don't know how you managed it at such short notice, but the security company is here already.'

He didn't say anything and her scalp started to prickle with self-consciousness.

'Rico?' The self-consciousness turned into something more sinister. If this was one of Chris's tricks… 'I…if you didn't organise for a new screen door and security system for me, you'd better let me know right now.'

She'd have to ring the agency to check this was all aboveboard.

Which was what she should've done in the first place! What on earth had prompted her to ring Rico? Because he'd made her feel cared for? Her throat burned. Hadn't she learned her lesson?

'The real-estate agent in charge of your block of units owes me a favour. I decided to call it in.'

She sagged.

'I'm afraid it'll mean a slight increase in your rent.'

She didn't mind that in the least. 'Well…' She swallowed. 'It was kind of you. I just…I wanted to thank you.'

'I'm just protecting my investment. Did you get a chance to read through the contract?'

She sensed his efforts to distance himself and it made her frown. Not that she'd expected yesterday's confidences to have made them bosom buddies or anything, but she'd developed friendships with all her other employers. She didn't know why Rico should be any different.

But he was.

She recalled the dark fire in his eyes, the way his hands had clenched yesterday when he'd said he would make a difference. She suppressed a shiver.

'I did read over the contract. I made an amendment.'

'Which was?'

'I'm not signing a two-year contract, Rico. I thought I'd made that clear. I changed it to twelve months.'

He didn't say anything.

'An oversight, no doubt.'

She wondered if he sensed her eye roll, because he suddenly chuckled and the sound filled her with warmth. 'Believe it or not, it was an oversight. Even though I *would* like you to reconsider.'

And just like that she believed him. After all, she had an entire security company tramping through her house at this very moment to prove the man's honour.

'It's just once I make a decision I like to get the ball rolling as soon as I can. I forgot to have that line changed.'

She reached out to trace the pattern on her teacup. 'Why does this project mean so much to you?' Why was this man so driven?

'As soon as the café is up and running and I have the figures to prove its success, I can start canvassing for funds for additional cafés in other parts of the city.'

'You want to run a chain of charity cafés?'

He blew out a breath. 'Why not?'

She couldn't think of a single reason. Except... 'Don't you ever stop for fun?'

He didn't answer that, and she winced at how it must have sounded—like a come-on. Her nostrils flared. *No personal questions! No curiosity!* Curiosity was only one step away from interest, and she *wasn't* interested. In any man. Full stop.

'Are you busy today?' The question shot out of him, as if on impulse, and suddenly she could imagine him without a tie. In fact...

She bared her teeth and cut off that line of thought.

'I know you don't officially start work until Monday, but I'd like to show you the premises we've organised and get your opinion on them.'

A tiny thread of excitement wormed its way through her—the first twinge of professional interest she'd felt since she'd been served with the papers informing her that Grandad's will was being contested.

'I'd really like that, Rico.' It would be better than sitting around here, stewing about the will. 'But the security company is here for another hour or so. At the moment I don't feel comfortable letting someone else lock up for me.'

'Of course not. And what about your car?'

'The tyres are being replaced, quote, "sometime this morning".'

'But you're free this afternoon?'

'Free as a bird.'

'Excellent. I can show you the café then, and maybe you could meet a couple of the trainees.'

Rico had certainly put together an interesting programme. 'Where should I meet you?'

'If you come to my office, say one-thirty, we can travel together.'

'I'll be there.'

'And, Neen?' he said, before she could ring off. 'How did your dinner go last night? The one you were stressed about?'

Her stomach clenched and roiled, although it touched her that he'd remembered. Last night had been an unmitigated disaster and—

'Neen?'

She shook herself and did what she could to inject humour into her voice. 'Given the week I've had, it went exactly as expected.'

Utterly, *utterly* dreadfully.

'I'm sorry to hear that.' He was silent for several seconds. 'Still, the week hasn't been a complete loss. Don't forget you *did* score an interesting job.'

Her lips lifted. 'There is that,' she agreed, before they rang off.

An 'interesting job', huh?

She sighed and poured herself another cup of tea. Time would tell, and even if it did prove true it didn't make up for not being able to follow her heart's desire and open her own café.

You didn't apply for the job as consolation. You

applied to stop yourself from moping and twiddling your fingers.

She pressed her hands together tightly. Hopefully soon enough she could put all her dreams into action. She stared up at the sky. 'Fingers crossed, Grandad,' she whispered.

'We've been given these premises on a two-year lease for practically peanuts,' Rico said as he unlocked the door to the Battery Point property.

'How on earth did you manage that *here*?' Neen breathed. 'It's almost waterfront, and just a couple of streets away from Salamanca Markets.' She glanced up and down the street. 'The rents around here are outrageous!' She knew because she'd checked.

Rico just shrugged.

The man was a miracle worker. 'You called in a favour, right?' If he weren't careful, he'd run out of those.

'The owner of this property is the manager of a local dairy farm. I've promised him a lot of advertising—on the flyers announcing the café's opening as well as on the menus.'

'Good PR.'

Rico switched on the lights. 'That's what he thought.'

Neen took in the size of the generous front room, with its two lovely bay windows overlooking the street. It was a pity it didn't have water views, although she supposed if it had he could have kissed his cheap rent goodbye.

'Obviously I said we'd do whatever maintenance was necessary.'

There was certainly a lot of cleaning up to do.

'What do you think?'

'I think we can make this look charming. All it needs is a lick of paint and some elbow grease.' She stepped back. 'It looks as if we could seat sixty in here comfortably.'

'That's what I was hoping you'd say. Come and check out the kitchen.'

She trailed a hand across the wooden counter and display case that ran the length of the back wall. She could imagine it polished and gleaming, housing a vast array of cakes and slices to tempt and delight. A smile built inside her. That cabinet was perfect. She couldn't have chosen better for her dream café, and—

She straightened, shook herself and followed Rico through to the kitchen.

It was smaller than she'd hoped. 'Have you had an occupational health and safety check completed yet?'

'Not yet, why?' he barked, spinning around. 'Do you see any potential problems?'

She pointed. 'Exposed wiring there, there and there…and that power point looks like a fire hazard.'

He swore.

'I'm not feeling particularly confident about the safety of that ceiling fan either.'

He glared at the ceiling.

'Still, the ovens look as if they'll be okay once they're cleaned up.' She opened a cupboard door and grimaced as a cockroach scuttled away. 'It's far too dark in here, and that's going to be a real issue. We'll need strip lighting all the way along here. We need to see properly. I can't risk anyone's safety around hot stoves and sharp knives. I wouldn't risk fully-trained, experienced staff, let alone novices.'

'The boys will learn!'

'Of course they will.' She wiped a finger along a bench and inspected her finger with a grimace. 'But they'll learn much quicker and more safely with proper lighting.'

He blew out a breath. 'That'll cost a fortune.'

She eased back and folded her arms. 'Did you ask me here for my honest opinion or to pat you on the back and tell you what a fabulous job you're doing?'

He stuck out his jaw and glared. She could see that behind the glare he was frantically calculating the budget he had to work with. 'That peanut rent suddenly makes a lot of sense,' he growled.

'How much are you paying?'

He told her and she shrugged. 'We're smack-bang in the middle of Hobart's tourist hub. You're still getting a great deal.'

He didn't say anything. She wasn't even sure he'd heard her.

'What's out that way?'

He shook himself. 'Storeroom, staff bathroom and the back door.'

He led the way, throwing open the storeroom door as he passed. Something furry brushed past her ankles. She let out a little scream.

Rico swung to her. 'Wha—?'

'Out the back door. *Now*!'

She pushed him all the way out into the cement courtyard, then stamped her feet up and down three times and shuddered twice. 'Yuck!'

Rico stared at her as if she'd lost her senses. 'What on earth are you doing?'

She stabbed a finger at him. 'I can deal with mice, and I'm even prepared to take a shoe to a cockroach, but I absolutely and utterly draw the line at rats!'

His face darkened. 'There aren't any rats.'

'Oh, no?' She pointed behind him. 'Then what do you call that thing creeping down the back steps?'

CHAPTER THREE

RICO SWORE ONCE, violently. The rodent scuttled down the steps and slunk behind some garbage bins.

A rat. *A goddamn rat!* The Health Department would have a field day with that. For a moment his vision of a thriving chain of charity cafés blurred and threatened to slip out of reach. Unless...

He glanced at Neen. Unless he could convince her to keep her pretty mouth shut about the incident. Unless he could—

He broke off his thoughts to drag a hand down his face. What on earth was he thinking? He couldn't put the public's health at risk like that. Besides, that kind of scandal would scupper all his plans. But...

His head dropped. His shoulders sagged. He was so darn tired of fighting for every allowance, for every penny of government money, for every—

He stiffened. *Get over yourself, D'Angelo! You have nothing to complain about.*

All-too-familiar bile filled his mouth. He lifted his head and pushed his shoulders back to find Neen surveying him with narrowed eyes and pursed lips.

His gut clenched. Then a car backfired and she jumped and whirled around. She turned back, patting her chest. 'Rodents make me jumpy,' she said with a weak smile.

His lip curled. Rodents of the ex-boyfriend variety.

'Are you up to date on your tetanus shots?'

That threw him. 'Yes.'

She pointed at the door. 'Then you can go back through there, switch off the lights and lock up. I'll meet you out the front.' She headed for the gate. 'Oh, and grab my handbag, please? It's on the counter in the kitchen.'

And then she disappeared.

Scowling, he did as she'd asked and met her on the footpath in front of the café. He handed over her handbag and tried to think of something encouraging to say but couldn't think of a single thing. Her eyes were too bright, too perceptive. She'd witnessed his moment of despair and it didn't matter how much he wished she hadn't. It was too late now—he didn't have the energy to make light of rats or cockroaches or dodgy wiring.

He went to unlock the car, but she shook her head and took his arm. 'C'mon.'

'Where are we going?'

'We're having an emergency meeting.'

'A…? Where?'

'At the pub around the corner.'

'But…'

She stopped and kinked an eyebrow at him. 'But what?'

He didn't know. Just...*but*.

She let go of his arm and kept walking, but he noticed the way she scanned the surroundings. As if waiting for something unpleasant to jump out at her.

He hesitated for a fraction of a moment before setting off after her. 'I have work to do.'

She raised an eyebrow. 'Ain't that the truth?'

A weight fell onto his shoulders so heavy he thought it might flatten him into the ground.

'And excuse me if I correct you, Rico, but *we* have work to do.'

The weight eased a fraction. He moved forward to open the pub door for her. 'What would you like to drink?'

She lifted her chin, her eyes almost daring him to contradict her. 'It's been a hell of a week, and I'm thirsty.'

He couldn't have explained why, but his lips started to twitch. 'A schooner of their finest?'

She smiled. 'You better make it a light. I don't want to go all giggly and stupid. And a packet of crisps—salt and vinegar. I'll be over there.' She pointed to a table in the corner.

When he returned, he found her seated with a pen and pad in front of her. She sipped the beer he handed her. She tore open the packet of crisps and crunched one.

'Okay, we need to make a list of what needs doing and prioritise it.'

He set his lemon squash on the table with a thump. Rather than despair, he should have started troubleshooting—like Neen. He should have been proactive. He was usually so—

Louis's birthday. He fell into a chair. Today should have been Louis's birthday, and the knowledge had taunted him from the moment he'd opened his eyes that morning, surrounding him in darkness and a morass of self-loathing.

He jerked in his seat when he found himself the subject of Neen's scrutiny again.

'When was the last time you had a decent night's sleep?' she asked.

Ten years ago.

The unbidden answer made him flinch. He stared back at her and ferociously cut off that line of thought. 'I could ask the same of you,' he said, noting the dark circles under her eyes.

A shadow flitted across her face and he immediately wished the words unsaid. Some jerk was harassing her. Of course that would be playing havoc with her peace of mind. Then there was that dinner of hers last night, which obviously hadn't gone well. The last thing she needed was to be reminded of her troubles.

'What happened at dinner last night?'

He couldn't believe he'd asked. He stiffened, seized his squash and took a gulp, almost choking on it. She raised an eyebrow and he couldn't tell if she was laughing at him or not.

'Sorry, none of my business.'

'It ended in accusations and angry words.' She shrugged. 'Which is what I expected. But a girl can hope, can't she?'

His hand tightened about his glass. Very carefully he set it down. 'You didn't entertain that ex who's—?'

'What kind of idiot do you think I am?'

Blue eyes flashed at him, easing the tightness in his chest. He frowned when he realised the tightness had threatened to relocate lower. He did what he could to ignore the burn and throb. *Louis's birthday.* It had thrown him off kilter the entire day.

'Sorry, I…' He shook his head. 'I've had too much experience with women getting caught up in the cycle of domestic violence.'

'Personal experience?'

'No.' He hadn't watched it from the sidelines growing up. He hadn't suffered from it himself. He had no such excuse. 'On-the-job experience.'

She stared into her beer. 'It'd be awful to see one's mother go through that.'

It was hard enough watching it in the families of the kids he was trying to help.

'Remember how I said there was an issue of a contested will?'

He nodded.

'Dinner last night was with the other interested party.'

And it had ended with angry words and accusations? 'I'm sorry it didn't go well.'

She shrugged. 'Thank you, but it has nothing to do with work. What we need to do is come up with a game plan.'

He was so used to people requesting—demanding—assistance from him that Neen's take-charge attitude threw him.

In a good way.

'I see the most pressing concerns as, one: getting the place fumigated, and two: getting in an electrician to check the place over. Rats will gnaw through anything.'

'I know a good electrician who'll be happy to help in return for a bit of advertising.'

She wrinkled her nose. 'Precisely how big are we going to make our menus, Rico?'

That surprised a laugh out of him. 'I don't have any contacts in the pest-control industry.' Though whichever company he selected he could talk to them about taking on an apprentice or two, couldn't he? There might just be a silver lining in all of this, after all.

'You're obviously worried about the budget.'

She lifted her beer to her lips and it suddenly struck him how pretty she was. Not in a loud, showy way—nobody would ever call her beautiful—but with her fall of thick chestnut hair, pert nose and wide mouth she was most definitely pretty.

And the longer he stared at her the more that weight on his shoulders lifted.

She touched her face. 'What?'

What was he doing? He didn't have time to consider a woman's finer attributes. He didn't have time for romance. Certainly not with an employee. He was tired, that was all. He brushed a hand across his eyes. He hadn't had a holiday in…

Ten years.

'Worry about budgets goes with the territory,' he bit out.

Behind the blue of her eyes her mind clearly raced. She had lovely eyes—not too big and not too small, but perfectly spaced and—

He dragged his gaze away. This woman didn't miss a trick, and he would not be caught out staring at her again.

'Look, this is a charity café, right? It's a programme to help train disadvantaged youth and place them in the workforce, yes? Then there must be huge scope to get the community behind it.'

'Every single charity and community service initiative can make that exact same claim.' He sat back. This was one of the major problems he faced—getting good exposure for his programmes, finding backing and sponsorship. 'The community is feeling a bit…' he grimaced '…a *lot* "charitied out".

People only have so much to give.' And they were asked to give to so many different causes.

He understood that. He even empathised. But if he could just get a few more key players interested... The problem was, his kids weren't cute and cuddly. They were scowling, slouchy, smart-mouthed teenagers. That didn't do him any favours in the advertising stakes.

Neen tapped the table with her pen. 'Earlier in the year there was a family whose home was severely damaged by a storm. Unbeknownst to them it wasn't covered in their insurance.'

He scowled. Rotten insurance companies.

'One of the local radio stations put a call out to tradesmen for help and they were flooded with offers. Apparently the advertising the tradesmen received was worth the work they did. We could do something similar. We could create a bewitchingly irresistible press release and send it in to the station of our choice.'

That had potential. 'I have a contact at one of the radio stations.' His heart started to thump. If they could get a fumigator and an electrician free...

For a moment he was tempted to seize her face in his hands and kiss her. He took a gulp of his drink instead.

She shimmied in her chair, her eyes bright. 'Do you have a contact at the local television station?'

Why wasn't *he* the one bubbling over with ideas? Once upon a time... He shook the thought off.

'You're thinking of getting someone to interview me, you, some of the staff?'

'I'd prefer to remain in the background.'

He remembered her ex-boyfriend and beneath the table his hand clenched. 'Right.' He frowned. 'Look, I've spoken to the press a lot, Neen, and I have no problem with that, but some of the boys are barely articulate.' If they did a television interview they'd need to show the boys to their advantage or they'd be doing more harm than good.

Her lip curled. 'Aren't you sick of all those earnest ad campaigns?'

He shrugged. All he knew was if you stuck a puppy, kitten or a baby in front of a camera you received ten times more funding.

'Why couldn't we do something fun? Use humour?'

He recognised the fire in her eyes and momentarily envied it. 'Like...?'

She suddenly laughed, and it hit him that she smelled of the crisp alpine air that could be found in Tasmania's Southwest National Park. A place he hadn't visited in over...

Ten years.

He swallowed and kept his eyes on Neen's laughing face until the darkness started to dissolve and lose its hold.

'Why couldn't we show a motley bunch of teenage boys walking the streets and looking threatening and scary, with a voiceover that says, "Do you want these boys prowling your street?" There could be elderly people rushing into their homes and locking their doors in a really over-the-top way. And then we could pan to the café, with all the boys gainfully employed and serving coffee and scrummy cake to all those previously scared residents. The voiceover could then say something along the lines of, "Help us get them off the streets and gainfully employed".'

Rico had to laugh at the picture she'd created.

'We wouldn't show them actually doing anything illegal. There'd just be a whole gang of them, and they'd be pushing and shoving each other and ya-hooing like teenage boys do. For some reason people seem to find that intimidating.'

But she didn't?

He remembered the way she'd bellowed at Monty on the beach and shook his head. Of course she didn't. He frowned, though, when he remembered the way she'd jumped when that car had backfired. Was that just to do with her ex?

'It'd generate interest.'

'It'd cost valuable money...and time.'

'But if it brings attention to your cause...?'

She had a point.

'Anyway, let's move on. As far as an advertising campaign goes, that's your lookout.'

He marvelled at her energy.

'I think once we have the occupational health and safety approval we should organise a working bee. We could do the whole radio call-out for help, but can you convince your teenagers to work for nothing?'

'Some of them, yes.' Some of them desperately wanted work, wanted a chance. More than he could possibly employ this time around.

'If they help paint and decorate the café I expect they'll start to feel invested in it. Especially if we reward them with free pizza.'

'That's an excellent plan.'

She sipped her beer. 'And one you'd already thought of, I see.'

It was something of a relief to know she didn't have a monopoly on good ideas. 'Promise teenage boys free food and they'll be there—wherever there is.'

She laughed. 'This is probably something else you've already considered, but...'

'But?'

'We *will* get tradesman who'll offer us their time free of charge—painters and carpenters—if we put a call out. Are there any likely suspects among your boys who'd welcome an apprenticeship in those areas?'

He was already on it, but... 'Darn, you're good.'

'I also think we need to build up hype for the café's opening. Could we raffle or auction tickets to attend lunch on our opening day?'

He rested his elbows on the table. 'I think it's a great idea, but I still want to open the café a week Wednesday.'

She pursed her lips, and he almost laughed at the way she hauled in a breath.

'So we're going to be busy next week, huh?'

'Flat out. I'd rather advertise a gala event for a couple of months down the track. I'd like to invite restaurateurs, managers of catering firms, hoteliers...anyone who might be interested in hiring our trainees.'

She clapped her hands. 'We could work towards a Melbourne Cup luncheon. That gives us plenty of time to get the boys up to scratch.'

And it would give them time to create a snowball effect in the local media too, with the clock ticking down the days. 'Excellent!'

He sat back. Instead of hard work and an endless round of bureaucratic red tape, Rico started to envisage the fun of the project, the satisfaction of achievement...and the knowledge that he could make this project work.

He could get boys with too much time on their hands off the streets. He could give them a sense of direction.

He stared at Neen. Again he had to fight the urge to reach across and kiss her.

He rolled his shoulders. Gratitude. That was all it was.

He drained the rest of his squash. 'Neen, I'm impressed. I knew the moment you walked into my office that you were the right person for the job.' Which begged the question, why had he ranked two other applicants higher? Why hadn't he trusted his gut instinct?

'But?'

'It's only now I'm seeing exactly how right you are for it. When you refused to sign the two-year contract I questioned your commitment, but I was wrong.' He sat back. 'Exactly where have you come by all your energy, your ideas?' Because if he could he'd bottle it.

Her eyes suddenly filled with tears. She ducked her head to hide them and his chest clenched tighter than a politician's handout.

'What...?' He swallowed. 'I was offering you a compliment.' Or at least trying to. 'What did I say wrong?'

The red sting took Neen completely off guard. She forced herself to breathe through it, though the effort left her throat bruised and her eyes aching. She gave thanks that the pub was dim and quiet.

'What did I say wrong?'

She was barely acquainted with this man, but she knew down to the last detail the frown he'd be wearing. She went to say it was nothing, that she was just being silly, but the words refused to come.

To be perfectly frank, she didn't feel like lying. Not to Rico. He might be driven, and wholly given over to his good cause, but beneath it all he was a nice man. He saw a problem and searched for a solution.

Except for that brief moment back in the courtyard earlier. Then he'd looked as if he could sleep for fifty years.

She glanced up and winced at the concern in his eyes. She didn't want him turning her into some paragon and sticking her on a pedestal titled 'Exemplary Employee'. She'd only disappoint him. She expected that enough of his job was thankless as it was. She didn't want to add to his load.

She forced back a sigh. 'You asked me where my energy and my ideas came from…'

'The question was rhetorical. I was trying to praise you.'

'I know, and I appreciate it. You made me feel I was doing good work, making a difference in a good way.' It had been a while since anyone had made her feel like that.

'But…?'

She leaned towards him. She almost reached out to touch his hand. At the last moment she pulled back, though she couldn't have explained why. 'Rico, my dream is to own my own café. For three and a half months I thought that dream was about to become a reality. I was scouting out premises. I was playing around with prospective menus. I got talking to people in the know about prospective staff. My mind was buzzing with ideas. But…'

She couldn't go on. Her dream had been delayed indefinitely and its promise tarnished. Maybe forever. And…

A weight bore down on her, threatening to crush something good and pure inside her. She stiffened her spine and fought the urge to drop her head to her hands.

'But it's had to go on hold while the will is sorted out?' he murmured.

'Uh-huh.'

'And my café is reaping the rewards of your disappointment?'

He *did* understand.

He reached out and clasped her hand. It flooded her with warmth and something else she couldn't name.

'Neen, it's only a delay. You'll get your café eventually. You're smart and capable and—'

'Rico.' She didn't want him to think she was wallowing in self-pity. 'I'm grateful for the chance you've given me. If, at the moment, I can't put my plans for a café into action, then running yours is the next best thing.' It would keep her busy. It would distract her from the shambles her life had become. 'I don't want you to think I'm not fully focused, or that I'm going to let you down. Regardless of what happens with the will, I've promised you a year.' She wouldn't renege on that.

'I'm not questioning your commitment, Neen.'

She nodded. 'I don't want you thinking I'm promising more than that either, though.'

He sat back. He removed his hand from hers. It

was only then she realised how much it had anchored her, and that made her frown.

'I hear what you're saying.'

His face had become a mask, and her heart protested at his withdrawal, but she told herself it was for the best. She didn't want him thinking she meant to take his cause up as her own.

She had dreams. People with causes would no doubt consider those dreams selfish. Acid filled her mouth. It was exactly what her parents had told her last night. They were too fanatical to recognise their own self-absorption.

She shook the thought off, along with the memory of last night's dinner. It did no good to dwell on it. She needed to focus on something else.

'When will I meet your boys?'

He glanced at his watch. 'I asked a few of them to meet us at the community centre this afternoon.'

The community centre? That didn't sound too bad. It was better than a skate park or a basketball court.

'Do they use the centre as a meeting place?' Community centres ran programmes, didn't they? She crossed her fingers. She really hoped Rico's boys were serious about working hard and taking this chance they were being offered rather than looking for ways to scam the system.

It wasn't a charitable thought, but she refused to get her hopes up. Disappointment had figured too prominently on her personal landscape lately. She wasn't opening herself up for more.

Still, if they worked hard she'd give credit where it was due. If not... Well, then, Rico would hear about it.

'There's a free gym attached to the centre. They use it fairly regularly.'

So no taking part in literacy or numeracy programmes, then? But she couldn't help noticing the way Rico's face softened as he spoke about them.

Those dark eyes of his suddenly narrowed on her face. 'I want you to give these kids a chance, Neen. They're rough around the edges, but they've had things tough.'

She raised her hands. 'I have no intention of prejudging them.'

He didn't look wholly convinced. 'Most people expect the worst of them. I try to expect the best.'

No wonder he looked so darn tired. Her heart suddenly burned for him. 'I hope these kids know how lucky they are to have you as their champion.'

He didn't say anything.

'How did you fall into this line of work anyway?'

The light in his eyes seemed almost to go out. 'There was no falling involved. It was very deliberate.'

She waited for him to go on, but he didn't. She swallowed. Right. She nodded once, hard, and reminded herself that she was an employee and nothing more. Even though she now had a brand-new screen door and top-of-the-line security system. What was it he'd said? He was *protecting his investment*. That was all.

She had to remind herself that she didn't find men driven by a good cause the least bit attractive either.

And even if she did, a relationship, or a fling, or anything the remotest bit romantic was the last thing she'd contemplate. She'd gone searching for love and look where that had landed her. She'd learned her lesson on that score, and nobody could accuse her of being a slow learner.

'Okay, then.' She rose. 'Take me to this community centre of yours.'

Neen met four of the boys Rico had tagged to work in the café. She was supposed to meet five, but one of them didn't show up. They mumbled hellos and were relatively polite to her, and respectful of Rico, but with each other they were rough-and-tumble and utterly foul-mouthed.

'What did you think?' Rico asked when they left the community centre forty minutes later.

She glanced at him. 'I think I need a coffee.'

He stiffened. 'They're not that bad.'

'I didn't say they were. Why are you being so defensive?'

His reactions to and relationship with the boys had utterly confounded her. He was such an advocate for them that she'd expected him to have an easy, big-brotherly relationship with them. Nothing could have been further from the truth.

Oh, each and every one of the boys she'd just met respected him—there was no doubt about that—but Rico held himself at a distance, at one remove from them, and she didn't understand why.

She shook her head. Understanding Rico wasn't part of her job description.

She turned to him. 'There's a coffee shop nearby that I wouldn't mind showing you. I wouldn't mind chatting to you about the boys and the physical logistics of the café itself too.'

He frowned. 'In relation to each other?'

She nodded, and set off in the direction of the coffee shop.

His long legs caught up with her before she'd gone three paces. 'I have no idea how your mind works,' he grumbled.

That made them just about equal, then.

'You wanted me to meet the boys, fall in love with them then tell you that your café plan was going to go without a hitch and be a roaring success, didn't you?'

His lips turned down just for a moment, and then the humour in his eyes made her pulse skip and dance. He looked younger when he smiled. He should do it more often. She couldn't help wondering why he didn't.

No curiosity!

'I wasn't expecting that.'

She stared at his firm, lean lips before snapping herself free.

'But it would've been nice,' he went on. 'Instead you've been imagining problems and disasters.'

She raised an eyebrow. It seemed he didn't have any problem whatsoever with figuring out how her mind worked. 'Along with possible solutions,' she said.

He stared, and then shook his head. 'Of course you have.' But he said the words almost to himself. 'Sorry.' He rubbed the nape of his neck. 'I'm so used to having to defend these kids that I automatically…'

His sentence trailed off. She didn't bother finishing it for him. She led him into the café instead.

'What do you think?' She waved a hand around at the décor while they waited for their coffees to arrive.

'Nice,' he said finally. 'It's charming and homey… cosy.' He swung to her. 'It'd be great if we could create an atmosphere like this.'

She bit back a sigh. That was *never* going to happen. 'Our coffees are ready. I want you to watch the waitress.'

They both thanked her when she slid their cups in front of them. 'What was I supposed to see?' he asked when the girl returned to the counter.

'She's tiny, right? And quite graceful?'

'I suppose.'

'Now look at the amount of space between the tables. It's small, yes? Now think of the size of those boys you just introduced me to.' She looked at him. 'I'd forgotten how awkward and clumsy teenage boys can be.'

'They'll learn!'

'Oh, Rico, will you stop being defensive for just one moment? I'm not saying they *won't* learn. What I'm trying to say is if we want to show them off to their best advantage we need to create an environment where we can do exactly that.'

He stared at her. He tapped a hand against the table. 'So when potential employees drop in to scope out the talent…?'

'Precisely.' She leaned forward. 'I think we're better off going for clean lines and fewer tables rather than this cosy country-comfort feel. We should take advantage of the history in Battery Point and do the whole colonial convict thing. That looks great when it's kept lean and spare.'

He leaned forward too, his eyes intent on hers. Dark eyes that could beguile if they chose to.

Her heart thumped. She doubted the thought had ever crossed his mind.

'Did you like the boys?'

Work! She had to keep her mind on work. 'Impossible to tell on such a brief acquaintance.' She frowned. 'Actually, I really liked Travis.'

He was older than the others, at seventeen, and had some short-order cooking experience. He'd maintained eye contact with her the entire time they'd spoken. She'd seen the hunger in his eyes.

And, like Rico, he'd held himself slightly aloof from the other boys.

'I suspect he's a rough diamond. If he gets the right breaks he could go far.'

Rico stared at her, his jaw slack. Then a light blazed in his eyes. It stole her breath. Before she could gather her wits he reached across, took her face in his hands and kissed her.

CHAPTER FOUR

IF NEEN HAD thought Rico's lips would be cool—
like him—she'd have been seriously mistaken. They
were hot. Searingly hot. Heat jolted through her all
the way down to the soles of her feet, electrifying
her. Telling her what she needed and how.

She gasped, but she didn't pull away.

His grip tightened. And then his tongue stroked
her inner lips, teasing and tempting, creating an aching space of need and desire inside her that grew and
grew and threatened every shred of her composure
until she thought she might die if she didn't respond.

Her tongue touched his. She felt rather than heard
his moan. He smelled of aftershave, but tasted
smooth, like a buttery Chardonnay. She pressed herself as close as she could and drank him in.

Beyond the sheer unexpected magic of the kiss,
the table bit into her ribs and the clatter of cups and
saucers tried to break her concentration. She did
what she could to block it out, wanting to savour this
one unexpected moment. A moment filled with en-

ergy and hope and a lightness of being that was utterly foreign to her but utterly right at the same time.

More china rattled and clinked.

Rico.

Chatter. Laughter.

Kissing her.

The sound of a coffee machine.

So right…

Wrong!

The word screamed through her and Neen planted a hand in his chest and shoved him away. She wiped the back of her hand across her mouth, trying to rid herself of the taste of him in an effort to settle the clamouring need that hurtled through her. Her body's betraying hum and thrum, its pounding and pulsing, made her grip the wooden tabletop in an effort to stay upright.

Rico stared at her, his chest rising and falling, his eyes dark and dazed.

She hadn't expected this kind of 'insta-lust' with Rico. He was so contained and driven. She hadn't experienced anything like it. Not with Chris. Not with anyone.

Chris. Ice trickled down her spine. She was *not* going to repeat history.

Her heart pounded up into her throat, but she forced her fingers to let go of the table. She slipped the strap of her handbag over her shoulder.

'I wish you every success with your new venture,

Rico, but upon further consideration I don't believe I'm the right candidate for the position, after all.'

She might need a distraction from her troubles, but not *that* kind of distraction.

She stiffened when he reached out as if to stop her. He noticed her recoil and reefed his hand back. His lips turned white. 'Please don't go, Neen. At least not until I've had a chance to apologise.' He looked away. 'Though I'm not sure I can explain that even to myself.'

The light in his eyes had disappeared, leaving them dull and flat. As if… She swallowed. As if the emotion he was fighting was destroying some inner part of him. She wanted to flee from the tumult he'd set loose inside her. She wanted to escape the recriminations that swamped her—run from her own compliance and stupidity—but… Those eyes! Whatever recriminations she harboured, he suffered them tenfold.

Composing herself, she set her handbag in her lap and gripped it until her knuckles turned white. 'You have two minutes. Explain away.'

He pinched the bridge of his nose. 'I've already told you I questioned your commitment to this project…'

She *really* wanted that dull flatness to be gone from his eyes. A bit of colour in his face wouldn't go astray either.

'Which is why I wasn't your first choice.'

She didn't know how she knew that, just that she

did. She wondered exactly how far down his list she had been.

'And yet you've brought something more important than commitment to this project.'

'Yes?' She tried to keep her voice icy, polite.

'A lack of judgement.'

She folded her arms. 'I'll have you know I'm incredibly discerning,' she bit out.

He stared. And then, incredibly, he smiled and the warmth returned to his eyes. 'I meant you haven't judged the boys and you haven't automatically assumed that this café is doomed to failure.'

Oh. She unfolded her arms. That was all right, then.

'You've brought a sense of...of justice to the table and it's bowled me over. You're prepared to judge people on how they act, not on how society perceives them.'

'Why should that be so surprising?'

'Because I'm used to working with people like me—we constantly feel as if we're fighting an uphill battle against prejudice and conservatism.' He scraped both hands back through his hair. 'I forgot there are people out there who are willing to make up their own minds.'

She shook her head. The man needed to get out more.

'I was sitting here waiting for you to say something cutting and derogatory about the boys, for you to tell me I was living in cloud-cuckoo land if I thought the café would succeed. Instead you came up with a no-nonsense solution to a potential problem and I felt…'

She stared at him. What had he felt?

'Hope.'

Her heart thumped. 'So you kissed me?' How long had he been slogging away at this thankless job with so little optimism?

'It was supposed to be a kiss of gratitude, but…'

She didn't want his gut-wrenching guilt to return so she kinked an eyebrow. 'But you were overcome by my animal magnetism, right?'

His eyes narrowed. 'Don't sell yourself short. You're an attractive woman. Even if you *do* try to hide it beneath those prim suits of yours.'

She blinked. She opened her mouth but no sound came out.

'I am truly sorry for my utter lack of professionalism. Like I said, I can barely explain it to myself. All I can say is that I'm mortified.'

'I can.'

He stared.

'Explain it,' she clarified. She sat back, narrowed her eyes and folded her arms. 'When was the last time you had a holiday? When was the last time you let your hair down and had some fun? When—' she poked her finger at him '—was the last time you had a break from work?' She'd bet he even worked weekends.

'I don't do holidays, Neen. I don't do breaks or

time off. My purpose is to make a difference, not loll about.'

Like her parents, this man ate, breathed and slept his cause. She suddenly scowled. 'Well, then, you'll just become another sad, burned-out statistic. Why don't you save us all some time and throw yourself on a martyr's pyre right now and be done with it?'

His eyes flashed but she ignored them.

'You're not Superman, Rico. Like the rest of us, you're flesh and blood. If you don't make some serious changes in your life you'll wear yourself out.'

'But at least it'll be for the greater good.'

His attempt to make light of it set her teeth on edge. 'Tell that to all the other female staff members you start inappropriately kissing willy-nilly.'

He thrust a finger at her. 'I can promise you that will never happen again. *Ever!*'

She tried to ignore the way her stomach dropped.

'Besides the fact it was appallingly unprofessional, I'm your boss! It'd be wrong of me to give you or any woman the impression I'm in the market for a relationship when I'm not. I don't have the time or the room in my life for romance.'

She blinked. Why on earth not?

No curiosity!

He dragged in a breath, but his eyes still glowered at her—which was far better than that awful flatness.

'Neen, you're a valuable asset to this project.

Please don't let my behaviour this afternoon induce you to turn your back on this job.'

She stared at him, and then she couldn't help it—she started to laugh.

'What's so damn funny?'

'You! You don't know if you even like me, and it galls you to ask me to stick the job out, but—'

'Of course I like you!'

She didn't bother calling him a liar. This man had no idea about normal human relationships. He was even worse at them than she was. For some reason that cheered her considerably.

She reflected on her brand-new security system and the promise of self-defence classes...and on the fact that Rico had been too much of a gentleman to refer to the way she'd responded to his kiss—that she'd kissed him back. She wasn't sure she wanted to, but in spite of herself she liked him.

'I wouldn't want to give anyone the wrong impression either on the relationship front,' she said softly. 'I'm not ready to test those waters again.'

'Duly noted,' he said, just as quietly.

She wanted her life sorted out. She needed to have something of her own to fall back on—like her café—before she ever risked her heart again.

'Well, as long as we understand each other then I guess you still have yourself a café manager.'

He slumped back in his chair. 'Thank you.'

But they didn't shake on it. Touching didn't seem a good idea.

'Okay.' She clapped her hands, trying to become businesslike and workaday again. 'How quickly do you think you can get in pest exterminators and an electrician?'

'Tomorrow—Friday at the latest. If they work the weekend the place should be ready for painting on Monday.'

'Excellent. Why don't I meet you and the boys at the café at nine on the dot?'

'If you make it eight-thirty you'll beat the rush hour on the bridge.'

She rolled her eyes and rose. 'Eight-thirty, then. And I'll be leaving the prim suits in my wardrobe and wearing jeans and an old sweater.'

He rose too. 'Ditto.'

The man actually owned jeans? She'd thought casual clothes might be relegated to the same dark hole as romance. She bit back the sarcastic comment that rose to her lips. What he wore and his views on romance were no concern of hers. *They weren't.*

'Do you have a photograph of Chris?'

She frowned. 'Why?'

'I want to know what he looks like. I want to be able to identify him if he starts hanging around the café.'

She hadn't thought about that. She swallowed and nodded. 'I'll bring one on Monday.'

He nodded. 'Have a good weekend, Neen.'

She didn't return the sentiment. She doubted he'd heed the thought behind it. 'See you, Rico.'

When they hit the pavement they turned in opposite directions. Neither of them glanced back.

Half a dozen boys turned up to help out on Monday. Their eagerness made Rico's gut clench—and, as usual, a familiar flooding helplessness swamped him. He *had* to get them off the streets. He *had* to find them jobs, give them hope. But he couldn't offer them all jobs. At least not yet. And it didn't bear thinking about the disasters waiting in the wings for them—drugs, alcohol, violence. And that was just a start!

Neen's brisk clapping hauled him from his morose brooding. He stared at her and eased air into his cramped lungs.

'What, precisely, are you hoping we get done today, Rico?'

He pushed his shoulders back. 'I want to get these walls painted. We'll need to polish the floors too, eventually.'

Like a lot of the homes in this historic part of Hobart, the floor was made of ancient Tasmanian oak. It would look great when they were through with it.

'But that had better wait until we've painted.' He grimaced. 'And the kitchen needs one heck of a clean.'

He was about to suggest they form into two teams—one for the dining room and one for the kitchen—when Neen reached down, picked up the buckets and detergent and started handing them out.

'Right, then. What we need is hot water, and lots of it, to wash down these walls.' She pointed. 'And those dustsheets need to be spread out.'

The boys began to follow orders, some looking amused, some jostling each other and tossing out casual insults. Rico was promptly handed a bucket of soapy water. He opened his mouth, but then with a shake of his head he closed it again and set about washing a wall, all the time aware of Neen and her take-charge attitude. He ground his teeth together. In fact, he was a little *too* aware of her every movement.

The boys made a lot of noise as they worked. At one point Carl deliberately jostled Luke. Luke tossed a wet cloth back in retaliation, and in the ensuing ruckus a bucket of water went flying, slopping everywhere.

Rico spun around. 'Pull your heads in! This is a café, not a football field. If you're not going to take this seriously then you can leave. Now. I have twenty more boys ready to take your places if you don't want them!'

Twenty? Fatigue hit him, but he kept himself stiff and straight.

Carl scowled. 'We were just foolin' around.'

'Well, stop it and grow up. You're damn lucky to get this chance. Don't blow it.'

'Keep your hair on,' Luke mumbled.

Travis, the older boy, glared and took a step towards the pair. 'Problem?' He cracked his knuckles.

Carl and Luke quickly shook their heads and went back to work.

Rico shot a quick glance at Neen, hoping the boys' behaviour hadn't put her off. She stared back at him. He swallowed and fought the urge to roll his shoulders.

She ambled over. 'I didn't picture you as the type to cry over spilt soapy water.'

He stiffened at the implicit criticism.

'This programme is important.' He glared around the room. 'I need everyone to take it seriously.'

'Right.' She drew the word out. 'And that means we're not allowed to laugh or have fun?'

He scowled. 'Of course not.' He glanced at Carl and Luke, both of whom had their backs resolutely turned to him. Had he been too hard on them?

'Glad we've got that sorted,' she said.

He suspected it was only an effort of will that prevented her from rolling her eyes.

From then on everyone in the room ignored him. That suited him fine.

As they worked, Neen asked the boys about themselves. Surprisingly, after a while the boys started opening up and answering her.

They didn't share the nitty-gritty stuff Rico knew about them—the broken homes, the drugs and violence, the poverty—they told her about their favourite football teams and what they liked doing on the weekends, what food they'd like to see served in the café. They told her their dreams. In less than three hours Neen knew more about them than he'd learned in three years.

Except for the nitty-gritty.

Eventually, though, Neen threw her cloth into a bucket and swung to face them all, hands on her hips. 'Okay, I've had enough. I've put up with this for too long already.'

Rico turned with narrowed eyes. Who'd stepped out of line this time?

'We're setting some ground rules right now. I was going to wait until the café was up and running, but I'm afraid I can't put up with it. And frankly—' she stared hard at the boys '—I think you could all do with the practice.'

The boys stared at Neen in slack-jawed astonishment. Their shoulders were starting to hitch towards their ears and their faces were starting to shutter. *Darn it!* She'd been building a great sense of camaraderie with them. It would be better to let *him* deal with this. Whatever this was.

He took a step forward. 'Neen—'

She held a hand up, halting him in his tracks.

'The bad language that has been flying around this room is appalling!'

Shoulders were unhitched in sudden relief. Rico's did too.

'Now, those of you who are going to start working in this café—' the sweep of her right hand took in Travis, Carl, Luke and Jason '—and those of you who eventually hope to—' the sweep of her left hand took in the other two boys '—know this. The moment you walk through the front door to start work you will mind your manners and watch your language. If I hear bad language when you're on duty here you will be out on your ear. You hear me?'

There were murmurs of 'Yes, Neen…' 'Sorry, Neen…' and 'No prob, Neen…' all around the room.

She smiled then. 'Thank you. I appreciate it.'

That smile hit Rico in the gut and the memory of their illicit kiss flared to life, starting a throb in his groin. He gritted his teeth and turned back to the wall.

He sloshed water over it and scrubbed extra hard. What on earth had possessed him to kiss her? He hadn't done anything that impulsive since he'd been seventeen years old and in all sorts of trouble.

He glanced at her again, and then turned back to work. He couldn't explain it, but Neen sparked all his latent bad-boy impulses and brought them to blazing, thundering life. Impulses he'd kept under lock and key for ten long years.

He ground his teeth so hard he was in danger of snapping them. Under lock and key was precisely where he needed to keep those kind of impulses. He couldn't afford to let them loose in the world again. They'd wreaked enough damage for one lifetime. He wasn't letting them wreak more.

Darkness filled his vision. Dragging in a breath, he kept scrubbing, and eventually the darkness started to recede.

He and Travis had just started taping up one of the bay windows when Neen came over. 'Travis, would you mind helping me unload a couple of things from my car?'

Travis immediately set down his roll of tape to follow her. As she walked past Rico, she winked. The warmth of it, the inherent mischief behind it, warmed the surface of his skin, reminding him of the sweet heat of her mouth and—

He promptly taped his finger to the window. He cursed under his breath. *Keep your mind on the job!*

And that was why he refused to notice how long Neen and Travis were gone. He'd finished taping up the windows. He and the boys had finished washing down the last of the walls. He glanced at his watch and tapped a foot. Before he could set off in search of her, however, Neen sauntered into the room from the direction of the kitchen.

'C'mon, guys, down tools. It's lunchtime.'

With whoops, the boys followed her out. Rico tried to hold himself back. He picked up the rolls of tape and tossed them into his toolkit. He snatched up a couple of cloths and wrung them out—

'Darn it!' He tossed the cloths into buckets and strode out to the back courtyard to find Travis manning a barbecue filled with sausages and browning onions. Stacked on a small folding table beside it were bread rolls, tomato sauce and a big bowl of coleslaw. The scent of the frying onions hit him and his stomach rumbled. Those nearest him laughed.

'C'mon, D'Angelo, show us what you've got.'

She tossed a bright green foam bat at him. He caught it and stared at her, nonplussed. What did she expect him to do with this?

She motioned for everyone to gather round. 'Okay, these are the rules. The batsman gets ten pitches, and the object of the game is to see how many catches you can hit. Every person gets a bat. Every person gets a bowl.' She held up a large foam ball. 'The person who hits the most catches wins. If an easy catch is dropped it'll be counted as a catch. Another way to win is to take the most catches. Everyone get that?'

Everyone nodded. Rico found himself nodding too.

'Oh, and if you hit a ball at the barbecue you'll lose five points and forfeit your turn.' She clapped her hands. 'Okay, let's go. Rico, you're up.'

Rico didn't want to play. He worked more efficiently if he kept his distance from his clients. Neen grinned and her eyes twinkled. He bit back an oath. Why did she have to start her team-building exercise with *him*?

He gritted his teeth and batted. And then he moved to the outskirts of the game. Everyone else joked and laughed and entered into the game with gusto. Rico couldn't help thinking of the phone calls he could be making, the work he could be doing.

He glanced at Neen and her laughter made him momentarily forget about his pressing work demands. It was good to see her laugh instead of glancing over her shoulder all the time and jumping at loud noises.

He blinked as one of the boys threw down the bat and shaped up to another boy. 'You didn't catch that!'

'Yes, I did!'

Neen stepped between them. 'Jonah, pick up the bat.'

'It hit the ground first!' He scowled, wavered and then picked up the bat.

'You *do* know it's to your advantage if he did catch it?'

'Yeah, but I hate liars.'

'In the café we work as a team.' She glanced around. 'We have to trust each other. Luke, did you catch the ball?'

'Yes!'

Silence for a moment, and then someone murmured, 'I thought he caught it.'

'I thought it was fifty-fifty,' said someone else.

Luke's chin unhitched. 'Really?' He frowned. 'I took my eye off it for a moment, but I thought I caught it fair and square.'

'Your word is good enough for me,' Neen said. She met each boy's eye. 'Just like everyone else's word will be good enough for me unless proved otherwise.' She halted for emphasis. 'I'd like you all to treat each other with that same fairness and respect.'

They'd all gone quiet. Rico studied their faces and

let out a long, silent breath. Neen had sure as heck given them something to think about.

'What if…what if we're not so sure about something, after all?' Luke mumbled.

'There's no shame in that.' She shrugged. 'I think before we swear black and blue that something is true, though, we need to be very certain of it.'

Luke shifted his weight. 'I thought I caught the ball, but if those who saw want to take a vote…'

'Nah, we'll let it stand,' said Jonah.

The game started up again. Not as rowdy, but with the same intensity. When the last ball had been thrown and the boys were in the throes of working out the winners—until it became just as obvious that no one cared—Neen hollered that the food was ready.

The boys immediately shot towards the table and started loading plates with sausage sandwiches and coleslaw. Neen even had a cooler of soft drinks on hand.

Rico didn't approach until the last boy had found a seat and Neen was in the process of spooning food onto her own plate.

She glanced at him and smiled. The exercise had brightened her eyes and brought out the colour in her cheeks—she looked all rosy, chestnut and utterly lovely. His skin tightened and his groin let out a long, silent whimper.

'I thought we were going to do pizza?' Her smile faded and he winced at how churlish he'd sounded.

'I thought this would be more fun.'

'You're right.'

She raised an eyebrow. 'But?'

'But nothing.' He seized a plate. 'It was a nice idea. End of story. Except you'll have to let me know how much this cost you. I don't want you out of pocket.'

She stared at him for a moment, as if waiting for something more. When he remained silent, she shrugged and moved to sit on the back step.

Rico made himself a sausage sandwich, spooned coleslaw onto his plate, grabbed a can of soda and then glanced around the courtyard. The only spare spot was on the step beside Neen. He hesitated. He could always eat in the dining area they'd just cleaned. Alone. He could make some calls... It would be the sensible course of action.

Some sixth sense warned him that Neen wouldn't let him get away with it, though.

He stiffened. Darn it! *He* was the boss here.

With a sigh, he plonked himself down on the step beside her.

They ate in silence for a while, but it started to grate on him. 'You're developing a nice rapport with the boys.'

She nodded. 'I am. You're not, though.'

What the heck...? He choked on his sausage sandwich. Fried onion burned a path of fire through his sinuses. Neen thumped him on the back until he stopped coughing and then tranquilly returned to her food. He glared at her. 'That's not important!'

She raised an eyebrow.

He lowered his voice. 'You, in effect, are their boss. You're the one who needs to be able to work with them and get the best out of them. I'm just—'

'The person who's giving them the opportunity of a lifetime?'

He couldn't speak. He set his food down, his throat too dry to swallow anything.

'Why do you do this job, Rico, if you won't even allow yourself to enjoy a tiny part of it?'

'Life isn't all beer and skittles,' he bit out.

Neen finished the last of her coleslaw and then dabbed at her fingers and mouth with a paper napkin. 'It isn't all doom and gloom either. I don't know anything about your background—'

Which was exactly how he meant it to stay.

'But I suspect these boys have more reason to whinge and whine about things than you do. Yet they still find the time to have a hit and a laugh.'

Her silly bat-and-ball game had been more for *his* benefit than anyone else's? His hand fisted. 'I'm not a charity case, Neen.'

'And neither are these boys.'

That left him speechless.

'They're individuals. Just like you and me. They have hopes and dreams. You can pigeonhole them all you want, but it won't change that fact. Yes, they've had a tough start to life. But they're not the ones in danger of losing their basic humanity. You are.'

She rose, then, and started gathering up the debris and urging the boys back for seconds and thirds. He watched her and wanted to weep. He could've told her he wasn't *in danger* of losing his humanity. He'd lost it ten years ago.

Rico's distance, his aloofness, his...*isolation* made Neen want to weep.

He was doing so much for these kids, and they were good kids. They were rough around the edges, sure, but like little children—and big dogs—they flowered under the influence of a bit of attention and quiet praise. And, as she'd discovered, with strict boundaries.

It didn't come naturally to them, but they were doing their best to curb their bad language. They actually seemed to like being bossed around by her. It made her want to hug the lot of them. And since Rico's outburst they'd stopped their playful jostling too.

She placed her paint roller in its tray, pushed her hands into the small of her back and stretched, taking the opportunity to glance across at Rico. He was really investing in these boys, and yet he wouldn't let himself enjoy a single moment of the time he spent in their company.

He glanced up, as if aware of her regard, and she stood trapped by his gaze. The memory of their stolen kiss spilled through her. She swallowed hard. She had to forget that kiss. But warmth flooded her and a taboo curiosity raked its fingers down her spine, making her shiver, and she couldn't look away.

He straightened. He rested his paintbrush on the tin of paint. And then he moved across to her with a slow, easy stride and her mouth dried and her heart pounded.

'How're you doing?'

She wanted him. In the most primal and elemental way.

She backed up a step, her mouth drying. She avoided buttoned-up executives. They didn't do anything for her. Besides, anything of that nature was strictly off limits.

Rico gestured around. 'I know this isn't exactly what you thought you were signing up for.'

He hadn't noticed her reaction to him. *Thank you!* She unclenched her jaw and swallowed. 'I'm fine. It's been kind of fun.'

He didn't say anything.

She couldn't help taking a swipe at him. 'I mean, I know *fun* isn't part of the job description, but—'

'I'm glad you're enjoying yourself, Neen.'

Which made her feel like a heel. 'Do you mind if we have another sausage sizzle tomorrow?'

'Of course not. I think it'll be well received.'

She refused to let a silence grow between them. 'Once we get the kitchen in order we can make pizzas.'

'Sounds great.'

He stared at her for a long moment and her heart thumped. She needed a cold shower—icy cold—and distance.

She reached behind her, seized the photograph from her back pocket and thrust it at him. 'Here's the photo you asked for.'

As if she'd snapped her fingers, his cool, professional detachment settled over him again like armour.

'Right.' His lip curled as he stared at it. 'Do you have half an hour or so to spare after work today? I want to introduce you to your self-defence trainer.'

'Sure. Thank you.'

Without another word they turned away from each other and reached for their respective painting implements. In an attempt to drown out the thundering in her ears, Neen started to sing a heavy metal song she suspected all the boys knew.

One by one, the boys joined in.

Rico didn't.

CHAPTER FIVE

NEEN VIEWED THE room with as critical an eye as she could muster. Which wasn't all that critical. It was impossible to be objective after all the hard work she, Rico and the boys had put in over the last week.

Décor-wise, they'd settled on a plain colonial style. It wasn't her dream décor, just as this wasn't her dream café, but…

The white walls, the scarred wooden tables and polished timber floor, along with the prints of old maps and photographs of Hobart's convict past, would be a hit with the tourists.

Just for a moment she let her mind drift to a light and airy Balinese-themed café with lots of wicker and tropical plants and—

A knock on the front door had her spinning around, heart in her throat.

Idiot. It would only be Travis waiting to be let in.

Instead, she found Rico. Her chest tightened and her pulse skittered. She stared at him for three frozen beats before she had the wit to jump forward and open the door.

'Hi.' Her voice came out breathless. And it took all her strength not to curl her nose in disgust at herself. Boy, she was pitiful!

His gaze narrowed. 'Did I frighten you?'

'Of course not.'

He glanced behind her at the room. 'Nervous?'

'Excited,' she countered.

His jaw dropped and he shot straight across the room to the display counter. 'This looks fantastic!'

He reached out, eyes wide, as if he meant to touch the glass, but Neen swatted his hand away. 'I just cleaned that.'

His brows beetled. 'Where did you find the time to bake all this?'

His hand was oven warm, and her fingers tingled with it. He smelled like fresh bread, which made her mouth water. She shook herself. 'I didn't. We're using a freelance caterer for most of these goodies. You're not paying me enough to cover the hours it'd take me to make those.'

He nodded, but when he turned back to the display case he pointed. 'That's *your* apple sour cake.'

Last week, while they'd all been working to get the café shipshape, she'd brought in a homemade cheesecake, an apple sour cake and a pecan pie as afternoon tea treats for the boys. And for Rico. They'd all been *very* well received. She'd taken the opportunity to show the boys how to cut and serve the desserts too.

She lifted one shoulder. 'I couldn't resist making

a couple of bits and pieces.' Making these kinds of treats was one of the main reasons she wanted to open her own café. She tried not to breathe him in too deeply. 'Once the boys are a little more experienced, and we work out what our bestsellers are, Travis and I can work towards whipping up the odd cake and tart as needed during the slow periods.'

'I'm hoping there won't be any slow periods.'

'Then you'll be doomed to disappointment.' Which, as far as she could tell, was the story of his life. 'Besides, we need slow periods to fill sugar pots, clean tables, restock fridges and all manner of things. The boys don't need to be flat out all at once to start with.'

She'd shown them how to make cappuccinos, lattes and espressos. She'd taken them through how to take an order. They'd role-played to within an inch of their lives. But real life could be very different from training, and she knew there'd be nerves to begin with.

'How long before we can go to seven-day trading?'

That pulled her back from staring at the way his dark hair fell forward on his masculine forehead.

'Do you always have to have your eye on dollar signs and the bottom line?' She moved behind the counter to fold a teatowel and tidy the laminated menus in their holder. 'Can't you simply relish the fact that this is opening day? Just for a moment at least?'

'I need this place to become self-sustaining as quickly as possible.'

Why? So he could dust his hands off and move on to his next good-works project? 'You *do* know that's going to be a constant negotiation, don't you?'

The current plan was for Travis to work full-time in the kitchen as a cook, with the other boys working a rotating part-time roster. The emphasis would be on training them as waiters and kitchen hands. It was all the budget could cover at the moment.

'If the purpose of the café is to train up staff and to provide a venue for potential employers to come see them in action, then…' She trailed off with what she thought was a self-explanatory shrug.

He glared. 'Then what?'

'If our staff are constantly being poached—'

'Gainfully employed by reputable employers.'

'Then we'll constantly be in training mode. None of the boys will be here long enough to train up as a part-time manager. So until you're prepared to find the money to hire a part-time café manager, we'll only be trading five days. And, look, Mondays and Tuesdays are traditionally quiet anyway.'

He swung away, and that was when she saw what was behind his sniping. Nerves.

He turned back with a scowl. 'I don't want the boys goofing off this week.' He stabbed a finger to the counter. 'You need to make sure they pull their weight. If you let them walk all over you—'

'I'm on it, Rico. I have it covered.'

She moved past him to let in Travis, who'd appeared at the door. She grinned at him. The teenager shuffled and sort of smiled back.

'Ready?' She turned to include Rico in the moment, and then with exaggerated care she turned over the sign on the door to 'Open'.

Rico glared at the door as if he could make customers appear by sheer force of will. He started to pace from one side of the room to the other. Neen patted Travis's shoulder. 'Why don't you go stow your things in your locker?'

When he'd left she turned to Rico. 'I understand this project is important to you—'

'No, you *don't*!'

'But the expression on your face right now is going to scare away the customers. Go and do whatever it is you do at the office.' She knew he had more than this one project on the boil, even if it had taken precedence these last few weeks. She started to shoo him towards the door. 'If you stay here you're going to make us all jittery and jumpy.' She didn't need to be jittery and jumpy. And she sure as heck didn't need a man who smelled of fresh-baked bread playing havoc with her senses.

He rubbed his brow. 'Sorry. It's just…the café's success is important.'

It meant *too* much to him, and she didn't understand why. It was as if his entire self-worth was tied to the success of this project. She pressed a hand to her forehead. Maybe he felt that way about all of his projects. And when they failed…

She pushed her shoulders back. This one wouldn't fail. She wouldn't let it. 'Go and do all your good deeds for the day. I don't want to see you here until after two-thirty, when the worst of the lunch rush will be over. We'll reward you with coffee and cake and give you a full report then.'

'Right.' He nodded and set off towards the door.

She shifted her weight from one leg to the other. Darn it! She couldn't let him leave with that care-worn expression on his face. 'Rico?'

He stopped and turned.

She moved to stand in front of him. 'Wish me luck.'

His lips lifted a touch. 'Neen, you've worked so hard I suspect you've made your own luck.'

He reached out and clasped her shoulder. Beneath his hand, her pulse leaped. His gaze rested on her lips for a fraction of a moment, his eyes darkened and then he stepped back, his hand dropping to his side. Neen almost convinced herself the moment had never happened.

'Good luck, Neen.'

And then he was gone.

Her pulse raced, her heart thumped and she found it suddenly hard to draw breath. She turned back into the café. This place was the distraction she needed. *This!* Not some uptight man who—

She cut the thought off and drew in a deep breath, counted to three. *Focus on the café*. That was all she needed to do.

Their first customer—customers, actually, as there were three of them—walked into the café exactly eight minutes after Rico had left. They ordered scrambled eggs on sourdough toast, and Neen rewarded them with free coffee. Travis scrambled the eggs, she made the coffee and it all went without a hitch. They high-fived each other behind the counter.

From then on they had a steady stream of customers. Nothing too hectic, but enough to keep them busy. There'd been plenty of radio advertising over the last week, and the warm September weather was luring people out to enjoy the sunshine, the parks that overlooked the harbour, and the harbour itself.

The day didn't go completely without incident. There were a couple of breakages, one spilled coffee and a burned pizza, but everyone took it in good humour.

As the day progressed it became apparent to Neen that the café would be a happy place. Maybe it was the way the sun streamed in at the two bay windows. Maybe it was the café's lack of pretension, with its scarred tabletops on display rather than tablecloths and fiddly ornaments. Or maybe it was the easy camaraderie that had developed among her staff.

In her opinion, the fact they hadn't packed the café with tables was a bonus too. It gave the room a sense of largesse and the tables a sense of privacy.

One customer had confided to Neen, 'I feel as if you wouldn't mind if I just sat here all day.' She'd bitten her lip then. 'Would it be a problem if I brought my laptop with me on Wednesday mornings and sat at that table there and worked for a few hours?'

'I'll reserve the table for you,' Neen had told her.

She peeked at her watch—two-fifteen. She expected Rico to show up at any moment. The boys were busy getting on with their duties. As a new customer came through the door—a rather large Italian lady—Neen glanced at Luke and he nodded, setting down his cloth and whipping out his pad and pencil.

Neen headed into the kitchen to unstack the dishwasher and ready it for another load. She'd just opened the dishwasher's door when Jason came sliding into the kitchen, minus the cups and saucers he'd been clearing. 'Uh, Neen.' He gestured behind him. 'I…um…'

He didn't need to spell it out. The expression on his face warned her there was a problem. She sent him an encouraging smile and headed out to the dining area. She hadn't heard the sound of breaking china, or screams, or—

She pulled up short when she saw the Italian woman haranguing Luke. Her maternal instincts ruffled up in an instant. Still, she made herself smile as she bustled over. 'Hello, I'm Neen, the manager. Is there a problem?'

'You employ criminals and delinquents!'

She glanced at Luke. He stared back at her, jaw set and eyes blazing. 'I only asked if I could take her order. I didn't do anything wrong.'

'Have you ever met this lady before, Luke?'

'Don't speak as if I'm not here!' the woman exclaimed.

'No, never seen her before in my life. I don't know what her problem is.'

Neen took the pad and pen from him. 'Thank you, Luke. I'd appreciate it if you could give Travis a hand out the back.'

Luke barely nodded, but he did as she asked. Neen turned back to the woman. 'Would you like to tell me what the problem is, madam?'

'The problem is your café employs criminals!'

Neen drew herself up. 'We most certainly do not. We provide training for youth who haven't had the advantages that other young people enjoy. My staff work hard and are bright and energetic. I'm proud of them.'

The woman stood and towered over Neen. There was something familiar about her eyes. Neen tried to reach for what it was but it slipped away. 'You should be employing *good* boys. Boys that your customers won't be afraid will mug them or steal from them.'

'My boys will do no such thing! Madam, you chose to come into this café knowing precisely what kind of programme we're running here. Nobody twisted your arm behind your back and forced you inside.'

The woman's jaw dropped. 'Are you telling me you don't want my custom?'

Neen slammed the pad and pen to the table and planted her hands on her hips. 'I'm telling you that if you choose to frequent this café, you will treat my staff with the respect they deserve.'

Rico made his way towards the café. He crossed his fingers and glanced through the first of the bay windows. Three tables were full, and he could glimpse more people beyond them. The clenched fist in his chest loosened its hold.

He opened the front door, stepped inside—and then froze. Neen stood four feet away, hands on hips, bristling and magnificent, and all he could do was stare. Heat flooded his veins. Hardness balled at his groin. He couldn't move a single muscle.

He forced himself to fight it. First he swallowed. Then he released his forefinger, his little finger and his thumb from the door to let it swing shut behind him. He moistened his lips. And as the rushing in his ears receded, he caught Neen's words—*treat my staff with the respect they deserve.*

His chin came up at that. He'd been an idiot, not putting this woman on the top of his list of candidates. *And you're not going to jeopardise that by kissing her again!*

He dragged his gaze from her to glance at the person on the receiving end of her rebuke and his chest clenched so tightly it threatened his very blood flow. He pushed a thumb and forefinger to his eyes for a moment.

Very slowly he let out a breath and took a step forward. 'Hello, Mum.'

Neen froze. She lifted eyes that had grown so wide a grown man who should know better could fall into them.

'This lady is your mother?'

He wanted to close his eyes again.

Neen turned back to his mother. 'You're Mrs D'Angelo?'

'I am.'

Neen suddenly pointed a warning finger at both Rico *and* his mother. 'You are both welcome to sit here, and I will get you anything you want, but I will not tolerate a scene—do you understand?'

'Of course,' he assured her, wishing he felt as confident as he sounded.

Neen refused to move away until his mother nodded her assent too.

'Thank you.' Neen retrieved her pad and pen. 'Please be seated and enjoy yourselves.'

They both sat and she started to move off. Rico shifted on his chair. 'You haven't taken our order yet. You don't know what we want.'

'Yes, I do.'

Just for a moment his lips twitched, because he

had the distinct impression that she wasn't referring to refreshments. Shaking his head, he turned to his mother. 'Hello, Mum.'

'Son.'

He bit back a sigh. 'What are you doing here?'

'I wanted to see for myself this café where you've been wasting all your time. I wanted to see the cut-throats you employ so I can identify them when you're found dead in some alley.'

Over his mother's shoulder he watched Neen straighten Luke's collar, lift his chin and make him pull his shoulders back. She said something that made him grin before putting a pad in his hands and pointing him in the direction of some waiting customers.

A giant hand reached inside his chest to squeeze his heart. Just once he wished the woman opposite had shown him that same kind of tenderness.

He met his mother's eye. 'It's not a waste of time. We're doing good work here. And, just so you know, these boys have never been in trouble with the law. They're not a threat to anybody.'

Least of all to him.

'Humph.'

If only it was concern that had brought his mother here, rather than ten years worth of bitterness and anger.

Bitterness and anger you fully deserve.

He'd long given up hope of winning his mother's

approval. He'd let her down and she'd never forgive him for it. If he could turn the clock back…

But he couldn't.

Neen set two mugs of steaming cappuccino in front of them, and two magnificent slices of her apple sour cake complete with generous dollops of cream. King Island cream. His mouth watered.

She pursed her lips, folded her arms and stared down her nose at them. 'Well, come on, then. Try it.'

He didn't need any further bidding. He spooned up a large piece of cake and cream and popped it in his mouth. His eyes half closed as the taste hit him. He had to bite back a groan. This was even better than the first time he'd tried it.

His mother stared at him. He shrugged an apology. 'I skipped lunch and I'm hungry…and this is seriously good.'

She deigned to try a sliver of the cake and her eyes widened. 'You made this?' she asked Neen, the belligerence gone from her voice.

'I did. It's my grandfather's recipe.'

'Did Rico tell you I run my own restaurant?'

Neen stuck out a hip. That made his mouth water too.

'No, he didn't.'

'Would you consider sharing this recipe with me?'

'It'll cost you.'

Rico choked, but his mother immediately reached for her purse. 'How much?'

Neen started to laugh. 'Put your purse away,

Mrs D'Angelo. It's not your money I'm after.' She glanced across to where Luke was serving two milk-shakes at a nearby table. 'It's his first day,' she said softly, turning back, 'and you very nearly shattered his confidence. If you apologise to him, I will give you the recipe.'

His mother stared at the boy, and then down at the cake. She leaned back and surveyed Neen. 'Rico tells me these boys have never been in trouble with the police?'

'That's correct.'

She pursed her lips and then nodded. 'Send him over when he has a free moment. And then will you join us?'

'I'd be delighted to.'

'You're a good girl.'

'As squeaky clean as they come,' she agreed.

A few moments later, Luke appeared at Rico's elbow. 'Neen said you'd like a word with me, ma'am?'

In that instant Rico was proud of the boy. He was trying hard to remain professional despite Mrs D'Angelo's prejudice, but he knew it was a struggle for a boy who was used to fighting his battles in a different way.

'Young man, I owe you an apology. I jumped to some rather hasty conclusions and said some mean-spirited things to you. You're obviously working hard, and your employer has every right to be proud of you.'

Luke's eyebrow shot up to the ceiling, as if he couldn't quite believe what he was hearing. Eyes everywhere but meeting hers, he managed a strangled, 'Thank you ma'am,' and then, giving Rico a quick glance, went back to the kitchen.

Thirty seconds later Neen returned with a coffee and slice of cake for herself. 'I'm afraid I skipped lunch too.'

'It's an occupational hazard.' His mother stuck out a hand. 'Bonita D'Angelo.'

Neen shook it. 'Neen Cuthbert.'

Rico suddenly felt like a third wheel at the table as both women quite literally ignored him. He understood it in his mother—*I wanted so much for you, Rico'*—but Neen?

He glanced at her and recalled the way he'd sniped and griped at her this morning. He grimaced. Her skin looked flushed and soft, her lips warm and inviting, and a throb started up in his groin. He reefed his attention back to his cake and coffee.

'I owe you an apology too, Neen, for talking to your waiter like I did. But…' She heaved out a sigh. 'I live in fear of hearing Rico has been stabbed, or worse, by one of his clients.'

Her show of maternal concern was a front—he knew that—but it made him ache just the same. Behind it was a will of iron, and she was still determined to bend him to it if she could.

'I can understand that.' Neen shrugged. 'But he's

a grown man who can handle himself. I can assure you that the staff here are no threat to him.'

'I can see that now. Thank you.'

Neen sipped her coffee. 'Now, I'll write the recipe out for you, Mrs D'Angelo, and pass it along to Rico to give to you.'

'No, no.'

Both he and Neen stared at her.

'You and my son—you are friends, yes?'

Neen glanced at him. Her mouth opened and closed but no sound came out.

'You order him about as if you are the boss instead of him.'

Neen snorted. 'I try to when I can get away with it.'

His mother stared at Neen, and then at him, with a light in her eyes that he didn't recognise. 'So—friends, yes?'

He wasn't sure what idea she had in her head, but she could be a dog with a bone and he hated it. He opened his mouth—

'Mrs D'Angelo, Rico and I have known each other for not quite a fortnight. We're work colleagues first and foremost. But…'

His mother leaned forward so quickly she almost knocked Neen's coffee flying. 'Yes?'

'Well, he's completely demanding—which drives me insane—but…' She shot him a veiled glance. 'He's also helped me out with some stuff too. I appreciate that. So, yes, maybe Rico and I *are* becoming friends. But that's all.' She sat back then, and folded her arms. 'Do you want to contradict me, Rico, and tell your mother you don't have time for friends?'

'I would never say anything so ungentlemanly.'

Neen shrugged at his mother and one corner of her mouth hooked up. 'You certainly raised him with good manners.'

His mother sat back, a satisfied smile lighting her lips. 'Excellent! Rico needs a friend far more than he needs a floozy.'

Neen choked on her coffee.

'Maybe you'll get him to see sense.'

He closed his eyes.

'So, you will write out that recipe of your grand-papa's and bring it along to dinner next Monday night. Rico will collect you. We eat at seven-thirty.'

Neen blinked.

Rico leaned forward. 'Mum, Neen might have other plans that night.' It was one thing for her to order *him* about, but not his staff.

'Do you have plans?'

'Well, I...'

'See—she doesn't!' And then she glared at Neen. 'You do not want to try my cooking?'

To his relief, Neen started to laugh. He blessed that sense of humour of hers.

'I'd be delighted to come to dinner, Mrs D'Angelo. Thank you for the invitation.'

'Such nice manners.' She reached across and patted Neen's cheek. 'Now it's time for me to go.'

She rose and proffered her cheek to Rico, who dutifully kissed it. She glanced around the café once more and huffed out an audible sigh, shaking her head.

'Oh, Rico...'

He tried not to let her disappointment burn him too badly.

And then she was gone and he fell back into his seat.

Neen stared after her and then sagged. 'Wow, she's a force to be reckoned with. She doesn't approve of your job, then?'

He scowled. 'That's hardly news.'

'Chin up, Rico. "It's a truth universally acknowledged..." that our mothers are designed to embarrass us.'

'*Pride and Prejudice*, Jane Austen?' he identified absently.

'Pick the first line—it's my favourite game. I used to play it with my Grandad.'

There was so much warmth in her voice whenever she mentioned her grandfather it made him ache. And there was so much longing and grief tearing through her eyes now it made him want to gather her up in his arms and offer whatever comfort he could.

Which would be a very bad idea on more than one front. He stared down at his half-empty coffee mug. '"It was the best of times..."?'

He could at least play this game with her. He forced a smile to wooden lips. Too easy. *A Tale of Two Cities.* He opened his mouth to reply, but a great smash sounded from the kitchen.

He winced. "'It was the worst of times.'"

She rose. "'Where's Papa going with that axe?'" she growled. 'And in case you're wondering,' she shot over her shoulder as she marched towards the kitchen, 'that's from *Charlotte's Web.*'

He started to laugh. And then he turned his attention back to the cake. As he ate, the knot between his shoulder blades started to loosen. Neen had called the staff *my boys.* She was more invested than he could ever have hoped for.

He licked cream off his spoon. She'd called him a friend. Warmth pooled in the pit of his stomach. He glanced around the café and grinned. It suddenly struck him that he felt more at home here in Neen's café—and there was no doubt in his mind that it *was* hers—than he ever had in his mother's.

And just for a moment he allowed himself to enjoy it without guilt.

Neen pronounced opening day a roaring success. Same with Thursday. On Friday, though, right in the middle of the lunch rush, Travis received a phone call.

He shoved his cell phone back into his pocket. 'Neen, I have to go.'

She turned from the salad she was tossing. 'What?

Go where? We're in the middle of the lunch rush, Travis. We need you.'

'There's trouble at home.'

'What sort of trouble?'

He shot her an agonised glance. 'It's my little brother.'

Right. She pointed a finger at him. 'Give me thirty seconds.'

She marched out of the kitchen, told the other boys that they were in charge of the dining area and then returned and checked the orders neatly lined up. 'That's table four's Caesar salad and quiche?'

'Yep.'

'Okay, I have it under control. Go, Travis.'

She threw herself into keeping up with the hectic pace of the orders. Word had spread and the fact the dining area was packed was a good thing—an excellent thing—but Travis's emergency couldn't have come at a busier time. She just hoped the boys were coping in the café without her.

'What on earth…?'

She didn't even have time to glance up as Rico walked into the kitchen. She hadn't seen him since Wednesday, and every nerve thrummed in sudden exhilaration, but she kept her attention on the omelette she was making.

'Where the hell is Travis?'

'An emergency at home. Something to do with his little brother.'

Rico swore.

More orders piled upon the board. Finally she glanced at Rico. 'Your family owns a restaurant. You must have *some* kitchen-hand experience.'

His lips twisted with a self-mockery she didn't understand. 'Not a skerrick.'

This time it was she who swore. Still, he was her only option. 'Lose the jacket and roll up your sleeves, D'Angelo. There's no time like the present to learn. There's a spare apron in the locker over there.'

Rico amazed her. He was quick, deft and he followed her instructions to the letter. In fact he was brilliant.

When the worst of the lunch rush was over, she turned to him. His cheeks were flushed and his eyes were shining. Her heart stuttered and her pulse pounded. She'd never seen him look more...*alive*!

He bounced on the balls of his feet. 'What's next?'

It made her laugh. 'What? You've not had enough punishment for one day?'

'This is brilliant, Neen.' He clenched a hand. 'All this...the rush and the heat! I knew this had to be satisfying. I *knew* it!'

Rico looked more alive than anyone she'd ever seen. Her breath jammed in her throat. Heat trailed a path down her neck to her breasts...and lower.

'What?'

That was when she realised she was staring.

'You're a big fat liar!' She punched him on the arm. 'You do *so* know your way around a kitchen.'

His grin faded. He didn't laugh or even smile. He just stared at her with those fathomless eyes of his and a mouth that seemed suddenly vulnerable.

'My mother wouldn't let me within ten feet of the restaurant kitchen. And whenever she caught me messing about in our kitchen at home she'd punish me.'

Her jaw dropped. 'But why?'

He remained silent.

No curiosity! She swallowed. 'What about now, though? You live on your own now, right?' Surely a *little* bit of curiosity wouldn't hurt? 'You must mess about in your own kitchen when you're making dinner and whatnot.' She risked a quick glance at his face before sliding two slices of sourdough piled high with chicken, avocado and cheese under the grill. 'You *do* live alone, right? You don't still live at home?'

'Of course I don't still live at home!'

That was a relief.

'I buy ready-made microwave meals.'

She folded her arms. 'You never cook?'

'I never cook.'

The sparkle had gone completely from his eyes. 'Wow!' she finally managed. 'That's amazing. Because, Rico, you have a real talent in the kitchen.'

He grimaced. 'I'd appreciate it if you didn't mention that to my mother.'

He didn't explain any further and she didn't

ask any more. She didn't have the heart for it. She thought she might cry if she did. She merely zipped her hand across her mouth and tended to the toasted melt.

After Luke had collected the order, she forced herself to turn to Rico. 'About Monday night… If you want me to make my excuses to your mother…'

'You think that'll stop her?'

'I…'

His gaze gentled. 'You'll be a welcome addition to the family dinner, believe me. Also, my mother is an incredible cook, and you deserve to have someone wait on you for a change. I'd like you to come.'

She had to swallow before she could speak. 'In that case I'd love to.' She suddenly frowned. 'This isn't a date, though, is it?'

His lips twisted. 'Not a chance. Friends, Neen, that's all this is. I'll pick you up at seven.'

'Okay.' Friends? She could do that.

Rico unrolled his sleeves and shrugged back into his jacket. She tried not to stare at him but she couldn't help it. She remembered the way he'd come alive and she moistened her lips.

'Any time you want to drop in here and play out your dirty kitchen-hand fantasies, you're most welcome.'

'I'll keep that in mind.'

His lips lifted, but there was no answering smile in the dark depths of his eyes.

She tried to pull off a philosophical shrug. It

would be much, *much* better for her peace of mind if Rico stayed as far away from her kitchen as possible. But she doubted whether it would be better for his.

CHAPTER SIX

WHEN RICO LEFT, Travis emerged from the shadows of the storeroom. Neen had a suspicion he'd been lurking there for some time, but she didn't challenge him on it. Instead she called out a cheery, 'Hello! Did you get everything sorted?'

He sort of nodded, and then pointed back behind him. 'Do you mind if my little brother hangs out in the courtyard until my shift ends? I swear he won't be any trouble.'

She frowned, hesitated and then went to peer out through the back door. A bedraggled kid sat on the bottom step, disconsolately bouncing a tennis ball between his feet. Her heart stuttered in her chest.

'Wow, Travis, when you said *little* brother you weren't joking, were you?' His brother couldn't be more than seven years old. When she turned, she recognised stark fear in Travis's face and her heart clenched. 'Why don't you set him up at one of the corner tables with something to eat, a milkshake and a magazine or something?'

Travis brightened. 'Are you sure?'

'Of course I'm sure.' She went to turn away and then swung back. 'Travis, are the two of you safe?'

His chin shot up. ''Course.'

She sucked her bottom lip into her mouth. 'Why didn't you want Rico to know about this, then?'

'Look, things are bad at home right now, but I'll be eighteen in a few weeks.' He set his shoulders. 'Then I can take Joey away from all that and become his legal guardian.'

'Rico would support that.' He might not be warm and fuzzy with the boys, but he had their respect and, so she'd thought, their trust.

'If he knows how bad it is he'll call Social Services. Look, I know he's a good guy and all, but it's his job. They'll put Joey in foster care...' His hands clenched. 'Six weeks, Neen. All I need is six weeks.'

Her eyes burned. Sometimes all a person needed to get them through was one person to love—the way Travis obviously loved his little brother. The way she'd loved her grandfather.

And the way she'd wanted to be loved by Chris.

She suppressed a shudder and scanned the courtyard and the lane beyond. Everything looked normal. Nothing leaped out at her and said *Beware*. It didn't stop the hairs on the back of her neck from prickling.

She dragged her attention back to Travis. 'Can you swear to me that neither one of you is in physical danger?'

'I can keep us away from it. I promise.'

'If you get into any kind of trouble, will you promise to call me? You have my mobile number?'

He nodded.

She let out a breath, but it didn't help ease the tightness in her chest. 'Okay, then.'

'Thanks, Neen.'

'I think it's probably best for Joey to come here after school Wednesday through Friday, don't you?'

He stared at her, wary. 'You sure that's okay?'

'Absolutely.'

Eventually he sort of grinned at her. 'Hey, Joey, come and meet Ms Cuthbert.'

Rico turned in at a harbourside mansion in the well-to-do suburb of Sandy Point and Neen's jaw dropped. 'You grew up *here*?'

He glanced at her, one eyebrow raised. 'Where did you think I grew up?'

'Given your do-gooder tendencies, I expected the ghetto.'

One side of his mouth hooked up. 'Don't let my mother hear you say that.'

That smile… She swallowed. It could make her heart stretch out and bask in warmth. If she let it.

She dragged her gaze away. Not that she had any intention of letting it.

Still, tonight it was hard to deny Rico's magnetism. She'd seen him in his professional no-nonsense suits, all buttoned-up and driven. She'd seen him in paint-splattered jeans where he should've looked casual and easy, but somehow still hadn't fitted in. But tonight he wore a pair of sand-coloured chinos, a blue polo shirt and…

Her fingers curled into her palms. Tonight his potent masculinity beat at her. Tonight he was a man she could suddenly imagine spending more time with.

And that was a dangerous thought.

They snapped away from each other at the same moment, realising they'd been studying each other for too long.

'C'mon,' he growled. 'Let's get this dinner over with.'

'You're expecting a fun evening, then?'

He didn't reply.

It didn't take Neen long to warm to Rico's family. He had two older brothers—both married—who worked in the family restaurant and who were obviously very happy there too. As the manager of Rico's café, she was instantly considered a kindred spirit.

Rico hung back in the background and didn't speak much. She recalled Bonita's hard glares, the cutting remarks she'd aimed at Rico at the café, and didn't blame him for not talking much, for holding back. She remembered him in the kitchen on Friday, the way he'd glowed with life and passion. Why hadn't he been allowed to follow in his older brothers' footsteps?

She might be able to bite her tongue, but it didn't stop the question hammering away at her.

'So what do you think of my food, Neen?' Bonita demanded halfway through the meal.'

'Delicious! I've never had a better veal *scallopine* in my life.'

Bonita beamed. 'Ah, boys, Neen has a golden touch with the sweets. Ah, yes.' She waggled a finger at Neen. 'I've had my spies bring me reports of your cheesecakes and sticky toffee pudding and key lime tart.' She sent a sly glance at Rico. 'I might try to poach her for my restaurant.'

He stiffened. 'Don't even *think* about it!'

'I can pay her twice what you can.'

Neen jumped in. 'I'm committed to Rico's project for a year. I've given my word. And the work is interesting—I'm enjoying it.'

And it had taken her mind off her worries. It occurred to her that she didn't start so much at loud noises now, at least not while she was at the café. Her spare moments were filled with café plans rather than fear...or angst over her grandfather's will. She drew in a breath and reminded herself that she had a lot to be grateful for.

'Humph!' Bonita scowled at Rico, then transferred her glare to Neen. 'If you change your mind...'

Rico glared at his plate. Neen bit back a sigh. Why was his relationship with his family so strained? Oh, he was complicated, there was no doubt about that, and Bonita was certainly overbearing, but she and her older sons seemed to have a great relationship.

What had Rico done to deserve Bonita's unending disapproval?

'Neen, maybe you can talk some sense into my youngest son?'

Beside her, Rico stiffened. She wanted to reach beneath the tablecloth and squeeze his hand. It didn't seem fair that everyone in the room should be lined up against him. Especially...especially when he worked so hard and his job was so thankless.

She thought back to her brand-new security system and swallowed. 'About...?'

'About this ridiculous job of his!'

She set her knife and fork down. Rico had provided her with self-defence lessons, he'd given her an interesting job and he was making a difference to every single boy who worked at the café.

'What's wrong with his job?' Sure, he needed to pull back a bit, ease up and learn to relax, but couldn't his family see what an important difference Rico made?

'He works with low-lifes and criminals.'

She kept her voice steady. 'I'd hoped I'd already reassured you that the boys who work in the café are neither of those things.'

'Then they're the exception!' Bonita glared at Rico. 'He should've been a doctor. He had the brains. It was his father's dearest wish. We scrimped and saved and worked our fingers to the bone so we could put him through medical school.'

Neen frowned and tried to deflect the conversation. 'So…you didn't raise your family in this lovely house, here?'

'Goodness, no.' Bonita named an outlying suburb known for its high crime rate. 'That's where we lived. And when my darling Nico died I promised him I would send Rico to medical school.'

Beside her, Rico sat straight and silent. Neen tried deflecting the conversation for a second time. 'How old were the boys when their father died?'

'Rico was only fifteen.'

Her heart clenched. 'It must've been terribly difficult, bringing up three teenage sons on your own.'

Bonita's face suddenly sagged. 'I let them down. I failed them.'

'You did no such thing,' Rico said, quietly but firmly.

'Did you go to medical school?' she shot back, with such bitterness it made Neen wince.

Neen swallowed. 'I think to be a doctor a person needs to have a great desire for it. It's a vocation.' She couldn't see Rico as a doctor. His bedside manner would be appalling. 'Surely…' She moistened suddenly dry lips. 'Surely you'd rather see him happy doing a job he loves than unhappy as a doctor? And he's making such a difference. He's doing so much good for so many people and—'

'Do you think he's happy?' Bonita folded her arms and glared.

Neen's heart sank then, because the answer was a resounding no. Rico was *not* happy.

She glanced at him. Why didn't he say something? Why didn't he defend himself?

'I think,' she managed, 'that Rico is a grown man who is free to make his own decisions and that we should respect that.'

'You are a good girl, Neen, but you aren't a mother.'

There didn't seem to be much to say after that.

'Well, that was fun,' Neen said with a brisk clap of her hands as Rico pulled out of his mother's driveway and turned his car towards Bellerive, on the other side of the harbour.

He knew she was trying to make him laugh, but that was beyond him. He'd thought her presence tonight would put a lid on his mother's usual harangues. Instead it had only made her worse. And, as usual, he'd had to grit his teeth and let her vent, because there was too much truth in all she'd said. He had let her down. It was only fair he pay the price.

His hands tightened about the steering wheel. But Neen didn't need to hear about his problems. She had enough trouble of her own.

She angled her watch in the moonlight. A glance at the dashboard told him it was ten o'clock. The tiniest sigh escaped her.

'What?' he demanded.

She shook her head and straightened. 'Nothing.'

'Neen.'

She let forth with a gusty sigh. 'It's just that Mon-

days and Tuesdays are the equivalent of the weekend for me.'

Bile burned his throat. 'And I've ruined your Saturday night?'

She turned in her seat to survey him more fully,
but he kept his eyes firmly on the road. 'I know tonight was probably a nightmare for you, but it wasn't
so bad for me.'

He glanced at her. It hadn't been?

'One's own family is always more difficult to deal
with than anyone else's, don't you think?'

Her lips looked soft in the filtered light of the
streetlights. He dragged his attention back to the
road.

'What I was sighing about is that this is the equivalent of my Saturday night and I'm probably going to
be tucked up in bed by eleven p.m. I'm only twenty-
five. How tragic is that?'

He immediately pulled over and racked his brain
for somewhere to take her. She deserved it after
putting up with his family tonight. And she had de-
fended him. He couldn't forget that.

'So I'd be correct in assuming a late night
wouldn't be unwelcome?'

Even in the dim light of the car's interior he could
see the way her eyes lit up.

She shook her head abruptly. 'You have to work
tomorrow.'

He worked every day. Weekends made no difference to him. 'I bet you've barely been out since you broke up with your jerk of an ex.'

In the dark night she shivered. His hands clenched. 'Are you up for an adventure?' he asked.

'I...'

'The truth.'

She lifted her hands and then let them drop. 'I'd *love* an adventure.'

Rico had to bite back a laugh when Neen bounced up from the blackjack table, her grin set to split her face. 'I won! *Again*.' She clapped her hands and laughed. 'Oh, Rico, thank you. This is the best fun.'

She had colour in her cheeks and her eyes were brighter than he'd ever seen them.

'I've lived my whole life in Hobart, but this is the first time I've been to the casino and the first time I've ever gambled.'

The Wrest Point casino, with its plush interior and harbour views, was a Hobart landmark.

'C'mon, I'll teach you how to play craps.'

Neen had as much fun at the craps table and then the roulette wheel as she'd had at blackjack. Watching her laugh and seeing the sparkle return to her eyes unclenched something in Rico's chest. Neen laughed and he found it suddenly easy to grin. This sure beat sitting at home burning from his mother's recriminations.

He pushed that thought aside and concentrated on keeping Neen in an endless supply of chips, enjoying himself by proxy, holding his breath at each turn of the card or roll of the dice, her exhilaration when she won spinning through his blood.

'Drink?' he asked, long after Saturday had become Sunday and she'd finally finished the lemonade she'd been sitting on for over an hour.

'I'd love one.'

He led her to a vacant table with a magnificent view over the water and ordered her a glass of champagne. He threw caution to the wind and ordered a beer for himself. One drink wouldn't hurt.

One drink could lead to two, and—

He cut the thought off. One drink wouldn't lead to anything. He was no longer seventeen. He had a tight grip on himself now. He thought back to the way he'd just lost himself in Neen's pleasure, her fun, and gritted his teeth.

'Look,' she said, sliding the cup of chips across to him. 'We have more than we started with.'

She was right. He pushed them back. 'You won them.'

'But you bought them in the first place. Don't argue with me, Rico. I don't care about the money, but...'

His beer halted halfway to his mouth. 'But?'

'This—' she gestured around '—is precisely what I needed. I...' She turned shining eyes to him. 'Thank you.'

She tilted her glass towards him before taking a sip. His gut clenched as she swallowed, her eyes half closing in appreciation. The bubbles left a shine on her lips, and heat circled his groin in a slow, sensual dance.

She glanced up, stilled at whatever she saw in his face, and then her blue eyes turned dark and smoky. Her lips parted and—

They both snapped away.

Rico ran a finger around his collar. 'I'm glad you've enjoyed yourself. I've enjoyed myself too.'

Which was true. He hadn't cared if he'd emptied his pockets to ensure she'd had fun. And she had. He suspected her enjoyment had come from the novelty of the evening—of learning the rules of the games and the exhilaration of trying her hand at them. His enjoyment, though, had been completely wrapped up in her. Her simple delight had touched something inside him that had remained dormant for a very long time.

He clenched a hand. It would have been better for his peace of mind if it had remained undisturbed. But when he glanced at her, at those shining eyes, he couldn't regret it.

He cleared his throat. 'I know this is probably easy for me to say...'

She dragged her gaze back from the harbour, with all of its twinkling lights and the myriad luxury yachts moored nearby. 'Yes?'

He leaned towards her and the soft scent of musk tickled his nostrils. Very slowly he breathed it in and tried to control the clamouring of his blood. 'I don't think you should let Chris turn you into a hermit.'

She glanced down into her glass. 'I know. I just...' She tucked a strand of hair behind her ear and smiled almost apologetically.

Heck, she didn't have anything to apologise for.

'After I took out the restraining order, all the harassment stopped and I thought it was over and done with. To have it start up again has thrown me into a spin. I don't know why, but it seems more sinister now, somehow.' She glanced around the room, her shoulders edging up towards her ears as if she expected Chris to suddenly appear.

If he did, Rico would—

He dragged a hand through his hair. *Violence wasn't the answer.* That knowledge didn't stop him from wanting to tear the unknown man limb from limb. Ten years ago he'd have hunted him out and done exactly that. And he'd have relished it.

He'd relish it now too. And the realisation made him want to close his eyes.

That said, no woman should have to live with this kind of fear. Rico slammed his beer to the table. 'If I ever get my hands on that low-life, I will wring his neck!'

She gave a short laugh. 'In fairness, I can't lay all the blame for my reclusiveness at Chris's feet. Losing my grandfather has...' She bit her lip and glanced back out of the window for a moment before turning back to him. 'He knew about my dream to open a café. He encouraged it and told me I could achieve anything I wanted.' She smiled, but it quickly faded. 'We were close, and I miss him. I haven't much felt like going out and having fun.'

His heart ached for her. 'I'm sorry, Neen.'

'He'd been sick for a while.' She shrugged and managed a smile that speared straight through him. 'We had the chance to say all the things we wanted to and I'm grateful for that.'

'It doesn't mean you miss him any less.'

'No.' She stared down into her drink for a moment and then straightened. 'He'd be appalled if he knew how small I was letting my life become. It occurred to me tonight that I'm still going to miss him regardless of anything else I do. So I may as well do good, positive things rather than sit around feeling sorry for myself.'

He admired her strength, her spunk. 'This is the same grandfather who left you the legacy that's being contested?'

A shadow chased itself across her face and he wished he'd kept his mouth shut.

'That's all in the lap of the courts now. There's nothing I can do but wait and see how it plays out.'

He shook his head. 'You can't catch a break right now, can you? That jerk of an ex, losing your grandfather and now this issue with the will.' He scowled. No doubt by some avaricious long-lost relation who hadn't even known the poor man but who was more than happy to turn up at the hint of money.

Neen suddenly laughed. 'I do, however—as you've pointed out on numerous occasions—have an interesting job.'

It wasn't her dream café, though. 'Are you enjoying it?' It was suddenly supremely important that she was. If she wasn't, he'd find a way to fix that. Somehow.

'Yes, I really am.'

A weight lifted from him.

She pursed her lips and leaned back, a devilish light in her eyes. 'Speaking of jobs... A doctor, Rico? *Really?*'

He tried to smile but found he couldn't. 'You can't imagine me in a white coat with a stethoscope hanging about my neck?'

She shook her head. 'I can see you in a white chef's smock with a spatula in your hand.'

He flinched. She hadn't said it to punish him, but that didn't stop him from reacting.

'I'm sorry. I didn't mean to—'

'Not your fault.' He didn't want her feeling bad on his account. She had enough to deal with. 'As far as my mother's concerned, a chef is a synonym for dogsbody.'

Her brow crinkled. 'But she's a cook, and nobody could ever call *her* a dogsbody.'

'It took her a long time to get where she is, to own her own restaurant. She really did put herself last to give us all a good education.' He scraped a hand down his face. 'She fought my brothers when they wanted to become chefs too.'

'So all her hopes rested on you?'

'My grades were good. And if it was what I'd wanted...'

'But it wasn't.'

The understanding in her eyes was almost his undoing.

She hesitated, and then leaned across and touched his hand. 'Rico, believe me, I understand the urge to please a parent. But don't you think it's more important to be true to yourself? I get the impression that once your mother sees you're happy she'll reconcile herself to the disappointment.'

If it were only his mother's disappointment he had to deal with. But it wasn't. He would never be able to make amends for Louis's death. His best friend had died at the age of seventeen and Rico was responsible. *He* was the one who'd bought the drugs with money stolen from his mother's purse. *He* was the one who'd offered them to Louis.

His stomach churned and acid burned his throat. He could never give Louis back to his family. All he could do was make amends the only way he knew how—do all he could to protect vulnerable youth, to prevent them from making the same mistakes he and Louis had.

He glanced at the lovely woman across from him and knew he wouldn't darken her evening with such an ugly story. But the longer he gazed at her, the greater the abyss inside him grew.

He wanted her. He wanted her in every fierce way a man could want a woman. But he couldn't have her. Even if she was as black of heart as him, he couldn't have her. He'd stolen his best friend's life. He had no right to one of his own.

Neen and Travis were cleaning up the kitchen when the doorbell tinkled.

Neen didn't look up from where she was scrubbing down the stovetop. One of the boys would see to the customer.

'Travis.' Jason appeared in the doorway. 'Can you come out here for a moment?'

Travis moved with a speed she'd rarely seen in such a burly teenager. Her mouth dried. Had his troubles at home followed him here? She burst into the café behind him and then ground to a halt, her heart racing. No, not Travis's troubles but her own.

Chris.

He stood in the middle of the room. Both Travis and Jason barred her way.

'Please, Neen, I need to speak to you.'

Her skin filmed with ice. Her need for love had put her in the most awful danger…and she didn't know when it would end. Surreptitiously she beckoned to Joey and he raced to her side. She put an arm about his shoulders as comprehension dawned on Chris's face.

'I would never hurt a child! And I would never hurt *you*!'

She couldn't help noting, though, how his hands fisted. 'You're breaking the terms of the restraining order, Chris.' Her voice wasn't strong but she managed to keep it steady. 'Please leave before I call the police.'

'Look, you need to know—'

He broke off as Travis stepped forward and flexed one large hand. 'The lady asked you to leave.'

Menace threaded Travis's voice and she barely recognised her mild-mannered short-order cook.

With an oath, Chris turned and stormed out. Travis locked the door behind him and turned the sign to 'Closed'.

Neen stared at him and Jason. 'How did you know?'

'Rico.'

One word, but there was a wealth of meaning behind it. In the end all she could do was shrug. 'Thank you.'

Rico stiffened, his knuckles turning white around the phone. Chris had shown up at the café? 'Don't let her leave till I'm there.'

'Right.'

He hung up at Travis's assurance, grabbed his suit jacket from the back of his chair and bolted for the door.

'Rico, where are you going?' Lisle wailed after him. 'You have a late appointment with that MP!'

'Give him my apologies,' Rico said, shooting out through the door.

Travis let him into the café five minutes later. 'That was quick.'

'I was already out the door when your call came through.'

Neen marched into the room, her hair gleaming in the single light that remained lit above the counter area. 'Travis, do you know where—'

She pulled up short when she saw him. 'Rico.'

And then a smile trembled on her lips, and for a moment he thought he might actually lose his footing. 'It's nice to see you.'

He shouldn't have avoided this place for the last week. Neen might bring all his latent, undesirable bad-boy tendencies to the surface—but that was his problem, not hers. A friend would—

He scraped a hand across his jaw. History had already proved what kind of friend he was. Neen didn't need that either.

'I'm heading off now,' Travis said. 'Ready, Joey?'

It was only then that Rico saw Joey, sitting at a table in the half-light.

He ran across to Neen and threw his arms around her middle. 'Bye-bye, Neen.'

'Catch ya, tiger.' She ruffled his hair, then handed him a paper bag that he held carefully against his chest.

When she walked past him to let the boys out and lock the door behind them her scent rose up around him. He pulled it into his lungs—a mixture of cranberry and coconut and something floral. Just breathing it in eased the tightness in his chest.

She turned from the door. A deep silence descended. He swallowed. 'Is everything okay there?' He nodded after Travis and Joey.

She shrugged. 'Joey sometimes comes here after school to wait for Travis. He's a sweet little kid.'

He pursed his lips. 'And yet I notice you didn't answer my question.'

She seized a cloth and gave the counter a vigorous wipe down. 'I'm learning that if I ask no questions…'

Now what? Did he need to look into Travis and Joey's situation and—?

A touch on his arm brought him back. Her lips beckoned, a dusky rose, tempting in the half-light.

'Rico, you do know that Travis turns eighteen soon?'

'So?'

She shrugged. 'I think he has everything under control.'

He hoped rather than believed that to be true.

'How long would it take you to assess the boys' situation, decide whether some kind of intervention was necessary and then do the relevant paperwork before sending it through to the proper department?'

Not as long as she evidently expected, but he took

her point all the same. Besides, that wasn't the reason he was here. He tried to think of the best way
to frame his question, but she beat him to it.

'So Travis rang and told you that Chris showed
up, huh?'

He eyed her warily. 'Are you cross with him? Or
me?'

'Of course not! How could you think that? You're
both looking out for me and I appreciate it.'

Her words, though, belied the way her shoulders
squinched up and the way her mouth turned down.
The sparkle in her eyes had been quenched and he
wanted to smash something. He drew her into his
arms instead, and pressed her head to his shoulder. For a moment she leaned into him, and it was
a sweet, heart-achingly genuine moment. But all
too brief.

She glanced up, pushed her hair behind her ears
and backed away. 'I appreciate the fact that you and
the boys have my back, Rico. It's just... I hate the
fact there's a need for it.'

Behind her frustration he sensed helplessness. It
made his hands clench. 'Have you called the police?'

She shook her head.

'We're calling them now.' He pulled his mobile
from his pocket. 'Chris has broken the terms of his
restraining order and we're throwing everything we
have at him. And if I ever get my hands on the slimy
bast—'

'Rico!' Her hands shot to her hips and she glared

at him. 'No bad language in my café. No exceptions!'

He glared back. 'Whose café?'

She lifted her chin. He immediately raised both hands. 'Right—your café. No swearing. Got it.'

He shook his head and bit back a grin. She was falling for the café. She was falling for the boys. Just as he'd hoped she would.

CHAPTER SEVEN

AFTER THEY HAD FINISHED filing a report with the police, Rico insisted on following Neen home in his car. He wanted to see her go inside. He wanted to know she'd shot the deadbolt behind her. He needed to know she was safe.

He'd thought she'd argue. She didn't. Maybe the expression on his face told her argument would be useless. Maybe she knew he was going to do it regardless of what she said. His hands clenched around the steering wheel. Or maybe this incident had scared her more than she wanted to admit.

When they reached her street he scanned the darkness for anything suspicious, anything amiss, but cloud cover hid the moon and the stars and even Mount Wellington. Rico parked and strode down the driveway to Neen's carport. He'd made her promise to stay in her car until he was there to open the door for her.

She shook her head as she emerged from the car. 'This really isn't necessary, you know.'

'Maybe not.' But it made him feel better all the same.

Together they walked to her apartment. Her hand shook a fraction when she reached out to unlock the door and his gut clenched. Blowing out a breath, she clicked on the hallway and outside lights. She turned back to him and bit her lip. From her courtyard, Monty started to bark.

Rico's shoulders loosened a fraction. Monty would provide another level of protection. 'I want you to lock the door, throw the deadbolt and—'

'Would you like to come in?'

The hesitation in her voice reached into his chest to twist his insides.

She moistened her lips. 'I'm hungry. I'm going to make a cheese and herb soufflé.' She chafed her arms and glanced back at the carport and then down the driveway. 'The recipe I use makes two very generous servings.'

Darn it! If he ever got hold of Chris... He forced himself to grin. 'Will you let me whisk?'

She suddenly smiled, and he realised she hadn't smiled—not really—since he'd walked into the café this evening. It helped unclench the knot in his stomach.

'You can whisk to your heart's delight.' She rolled her eyes. 'C'mon—I'd better let that loopy dog in before he breaks down the door or does himself an injury.'

Monty greeted her with all the delight in his oversized heart, whining at her as if trying to speak his love, rolling on the floor at her feet, licking her hands, her arms and her face when she knelt down to pet him. But not once did he jump up on her.

'He's a different dog.'

'Don't you believe it.' She rose. 'The dog walker you found me makes a huge difference, though. Especially on a day like today when I don't get home till late.' She sent him a smile.

Her gratitude had him rolling his shoulders. He hadn't done much. She'd mentioned in passing that she needed to find a dog walker. He'd just happened to know of a local kid who had more time on his hands than was wise and had paired them up. No sweat.

'This dog has more energy than is good for him… *and* me. Monty—on your mat.'

The Great Dane immediately moved to a mat on the far side of the kitchen. Neen gave him a giant bone, upon which he set to with gusto as if half starved. Given his condition, he was anything but starved. In Neen's charge he was thriving. Rico suspected it had a lot to do with routine and consistency and discipline. Maybe she was right—dogs and boys had more in common than he'd thought.

She washed her hands at the sink and motioned for him to do the same. She brandished a whisk as if she were Eve and it the forbidden fruit, and he couldn't help but grin. The mischief in her face momentarily banished the lines of strain from around her eyes and mouth. It eased the tension in her shoulders and back.

'Temptress,' he growled, reaching for the whisk, intent on keeping the moment light hearted and fun. Her laugh was his reward.

'I think Nigella has proved how sexy a woman can be in the kitchen.'

She swung away towards the refrigerator, nose in the air, and he had to close his eyes. Nigella had nothing on this woman.

She came back with an armful of ingredients. 'Have you ever separated an egg before?'

He gazed at her blankly. 'Have I *what*?'

She rubbed her hands together and grinned. 'Oh, we're in for some fun. I think you'd better put this on.'

She rummaged in a drawer and handed him an apron.

He did as she ordered, throwing himself into her lesson with everything he had, determined to keep her mind off Chris. But as he followed her instructions and created something he'd never have dared before, it was his mind that was soothed.

'Easy, wasn't it?' she said, after he'd put the soufflé in the oven.'

'I… Yes. It…making that…it…' He didn't know how to explain it.

'Making food like that feeds something in my soul,' she said.

That explained it exactly! Right now, in this very moment, he felt more alive than—

Louis.

And just like that everything darkened. What did he think he was doing? He wasn't here to have *fun*.

A sudden gust of wind rattled the windows, sending the branches of the grevillea outside scraping against the glass, and Neen almost jumped out of her skin. She tried to cover it by going to the fridge and grabbing a bottle of wine. Rico clenched his jaw. Chris should be strung up by the thumbs for threatening her security like this.

She poured them both a glass and pushed one his way. 'Surely you've tossed a salad before?'

'I'm very good at slicing cucumbers.'

He said it so deadpan she snorted in laughter. But the laughter didn't chase the shadows away, and every time she glanced at the window his hand tightened about his knife.

He cleared his throat, wanting to make her smile the way she had at the casino. 'You're a natural teacher—you know that?'

She glanced up from tearing lettuce into a bowl. 'I guess it's in my genes.'

'Your parents are teachers?'

A dark cloud settled over her features. 'No.' She shook herself and smiled, but he recognised the strain behind it. 'I was referring to my grandfather. It was him who taught me to cook. He was very patient, and never the slightest bit flustered in the kitchen.' This time when she smiled it seemed effortless. 'I've tried to model myself on him.'

'He sounds like quite a man.'

'He was.'

He sensed her grief but was determined not to lose her to it. She'd been through enough for one day. 'And he's the reason you want to open your own café?'

She nodded and suddenly laughed, and he couldn't help a thrill of achievement. It might not be her casino laugh, but it was better than anxiety and dread.

'When I was little I'd spend hours describing to him in minute detail the café I'd one day own. Mind you, the décor changed every second week when I was a teenager—from a pink fairytale of a thing to a dark, smoky jazz den.'

The oven dinged, making them both jump this time, but Neen merely smiled. 'Time to eat. You set the table while I get the food.'

She'd given him completely free rein in her kitchen and he couldn't explain why it felt so good—only knew that it did.

'Do you want to eat in here or the dining room?'

'Whatever you'd prefer,' she said, busy with a salad dressing.

They ate at the kitchen table. His jaw dropped when she pulled the perfectly formed soufflé from the oven. He stared at it, his mouth opening and closing.

'I made that,' he said stupidly.

'It's perfect.'

He sat up straighter. His shoulders went back.

'Smell it.' She waved it under his nose before setting it on a trivet. 'That's where the real proof lies.'

Every saliva gland he possessed kicked to life as the smell hit him. Somehow he managed to shake his head. 'Surely the proof is in the tasting?'

And he wanted to taste it. Everything inside him clamoured to gorge itself on this soufflé. He seized the serving spoon and then glanced at Neen uncertainly. Maybe she—

'It's the chef's prerogative to serve the food.'

He took her plate and spooned out a serving. He went to give her more but she shook her head. 'That's plenty for me, thank you.' She helped herself to salad.

Rico served himself a generous amount of soufflé. He ignored the salad. He lifted his fork… *Darn it!* He set his fork down again to raise his wine glass. 'Cheers.'

She raised her glass too. 'Cheers.'

He couldn't delay any longer. He lifted a forkful of soufflé to his mouth and held it on his tongue for a brief moment. Flavour exploded through him. He stared at Neen, unable to say a word.

She sampled it. Her eyes closed. 'Food of the gods,' she breathed.

He'd created this. *Him.* He suddenly had to battle a lump in his throat. It made no sense at all, but it lodged there, preventing him from eating for several long moments.

Eventually, though, the scent of the food dissolved the knot. He ate and ate. Without a word Neen served him more. He ate until it was all gone and he could hardly move.

Neen smiled across the table at him and he found himself suddenly ravenous again.

'Feel better?' she asked.

He did. He felt better than...than when he'd won a hotly contested government grant. Better than when he'd pulled a kid back from the edge of destruction.

His lips twisted. Which just went to show how shallow he was.

'Rico,' Neen chided, as if she could see right through him. 'There's absolutely nothing wrong with enjoying the fruits of your labour.'

She didn't understand.

'This—' she spread her hands '—isn't hurting anyone.'

Isn't hurting anyone? He stilled. The churning in his stomach slowed. That, at least, was something.

In the next instant he clenched his hands. *No!* It was *wrong.* Moments like these deflected him from what was important.

'A man like you needs to fill his soul, Rico.'

Her words chilled him. 'A man like me?'

'You're so driven. If you don't stop every now and again to fill yourself up, you'll burn out.'

He knew she didn't mean fill up in a physical sense, but an emotional one. He pulled air into lungs that didn't want to work. 'My job is very satisfying.'

'Piffle.' She rose and started clearing the table. 'Do you want to wash or wipe?'

He shot to his feet and carried the plates to the sink. 'I'll wash. You know where everything goes, so you can put away as you wipe.'

He turned on the hot water with a savage twist of his fingers and water shot all over him. Darn it! He mopped at it and then thrust out his jaw.

'Why don't you think my job is satisfying?' He endured enough grief from his family on that front without Neen joining in.

'Because you don't smile at work. You *never* smile at work.'

Her words pierced straight through him. He stared at her and didn't know what to say.

She reached over and turned off the taps before the water overflowed. 'You smiled tonight when you were making the soufflé. And you smiled as you ate it.'

He seized the plates, dumped them into the soapy water and started scrubbing. 'My job is important. It's vital I stay one step ahead of the nay-sayers and grant allocators.' He stacked the plates in her dish rack and then snatched up a mixing bowl. 'I have to keep my ear constantly to the ground in case I miss out on funding opportunities.' He dunked that bowl in the water too, sending up a spray of suds. 'I have to stay alert for the possibility of corporate partnerships.' His hand clenched about the dishcloth. 'And I have to keep those boys out of trouble. I don't have time to smile!'

'I'm not saying I don't think you're good at your job, Rico. I think you're brilliant at it.'

He blinked, but her praise didn't touch him the way it had when she'd told him his soufflé was perfect.

'What I'm saying is you need to do things you enjoy once in a while too.'

He turned back to the sink with a snort of impatience.

'Fine,' she snapped. 'But I want you to stop and think about the day you had today.'

She tossed the teatowel over her shoulder and reached into the soapy water to grip his hands and stop him from scrubbing. The movement brought her in close. Her scent teased and tempted. Her lips were so pink they made him think of frosting on a cake.

'Rico!'

He snapped back to attention to find her breathing was as shaky as his.

'I want you to go over the day in your mind—the meetings, the running around, whatever else you did today.'

And because there didn't seem to be anything else to do—at least nothing *safe*—and because she still gripped his hands, he did as she bade. He closed his eyes to block the temptation of her lips and thought back over his day.

It had started with a seven o'clock meeting with the manager of an ice cream factory. It had gone well. The man had agreed to sponsor a traineeship through his factory. Only one, but at least it was something. Then there'd followed a series of bureaucratic meetings in which *i*s had needed dotting and *t*s crossing—a waste of time that could make a mortal man with things to do want to explode. Next there'd been a round of endless paperwork, a call from a youth worker looking for advice on a particularly challenging case and the routine roundabout of worries and concerns that his job entailed.

A weight settled across his shoulders. He opened his eyes to find Neen watching him.

'Now I want you to think about making that soufflé.'

He opened his mouth, but she released his hands to hold up a finger.

'It was fun, right?'

Sure, it had been fun. He had no intention of denying that. He didn't want to deny it. But making soufflés wasn't important like—

'Close your eyes and think about it!'

To humour her, he did as she said. Making the soufflé had been… Well… He rolled his shoulders. Learning how to do something new had fired him up. The feel of the ingredients as he'd whisked and chopped, their scent and the way he'd felt so at home in Neen's kitchen…it had all been…pleasant.

He opened his eyes and gazed back at her. What?

Did she expect him to have had some great epiphany about changing the course of his career?

'Now tell me how you feel about facing your day tomorrow.'

He blinked.

'Do you feel heavy with care and tired at the prospect of all that endless red tape you'll have to wade through?'

He rolled his shoulders. Yes. The answer was yes. But... But it wasn't as bad as he'd felt this morning or yesterday morning.

'I think I've made my point.'

So much for having a poker face!

His heart started to thud. The thing was she *had* made her point. And now he wasn't quite sure what to do with the knowledge.

'I want to thank you, Rico.'

When he glanced at her she wiped her hands on the teatowel and then tucked her hair behind her ears.

'Chris showing up like he did spooked me, but you being here for dinner tonight and just hanging out has helped take my mind off it...helped me find my centre again. I feel much calmer.'

Mission accomplished. 'Anytime, Neen.'

Her gaze shifted to his mouth. She stared for a long moment, a sigh rippling out of her and parting her lips. She moistened them and hunger roared in his ears.

And then she snapped away and he was left clenching the soufflé dish and breathing hard, as if he'd run a race.

* * *

'When are we planning to go to seven-day trading?' Travis asked the next afternoon.

The lunch crowd had long since been dispelled and they only had a few late-afternoon customers in, enjoying coffee and cake while the rain turned the day grey outside the windows. Today the weather had kept most people indoors.

Neen glanced up from polishing cutlery with a half laugh. 'We haven't even been open a full three weeks and yet you're eager to expand our operations, huh?'

He ducked his head, scrubbing harder as he cleaned the coffee machine. 'I... It's just we seem to be doing so well, and...'

'And?'

'I really like this place. I like working here.'

Travis wasn't given to chatter, so this was almost garrulous for him. 'You didn't expect to like it?'

He glanced up quickly. 'I was really grateful for the job.'

Her heart went out to him. 'I know you were, Travis. That was never in question. But we poor foot soldiers *have* to work. We don't have the luxury of sitting at home with our feet up. But it doesn't always mean we love our jobs. And I don't think there's any shame in that...as long as we do our jobs to the best of our ability.'

'But you *love* working here.'

She frowned. She did, actually. She'd expected to

enjoy it, but not to love it. She'd thought the delay to opening her own café would chafe at her constantly. But it hadn't. 'Yeah, I guess I do.'

'And I do too. I love it.'

Travis's skill set was growing beyond all expectation. His skills had been pretty good when he'd started, but each week they'd improved, and kept improving. If he kept going at this rate one of the big tourist hotels would snap him up.

It hit her how much she'd miss him. Still, this was the purpose of the programme Rico was implementing—to provide the boys with training and then send them out in the big wide world. But...

'What are your dreams, Travis? Where would you like to see your career go?'

She waited to hear him say he'd like to be the next Jamie Oliver, or become head chef at some fancy five-star hotel in the city.

'I want to do what you're doing, Neen. I want to manage a café.'

She stopped polishing cutlery to stare at him. 'If the manager of Wrest Point Casino came in here with an offer to train you as a chef...?'

His face clouded. 'I'd take it.'

Because it was what was expected of him!

She straightened. 'I'm here for twelve months, Travis, and then I'm hoping to open a café of my own. If the Wrest Point Casino offered you the position I just spoke about and at the same time Rico offered you my job, where you'd be earning half the money, which would you take?'

'This one.'

'And the money?'

'I can take care of Joey on what I'm making now. With this job I can still be with Joey in the evenings and get him off to school in the mornings. I couldn't if I was working nights at some fancy restaurant.'

Her mind started to race. 'Rico hasn't told me of his plans, but if you want I can train you up—and when you're ready, if Rico agrees, we can go to seven-day trading and you'll be fully in charge for two days a week.'

His eyes shone. 'Really?'

'I'm not making promises, and I'll have to run it by Rico first.' She didn't want to get his hopes too high. 'But we can see how things go.'

He nodded, so eager she wanted to hug him. He was trying so hard. He deserved a break. He deserved to have something go his way.

A cry from Joey in his usual spot in the corner had them both swinging around. Neen's heart pounded and all her muscles bunched, but she couldn't see Chris anywhere. Instead a woman swayed from the door to the counter, where Neen stood.

'Nice 'stablishment,' she slurred.

The stench of liquor hit Neen right in the face. She did her best not to recoil. 'Thank you,' she managed, but before she could ask what she could get for her Travis had raced around the counter to take the woman's arm.

'Mum, I told you not to come here.'

Mum!

The woman pushed him away. 'Give me money, you ungrateful piece of—'

A hacking cough interrupted her flow of words. Neen closed her eyes and swallowed. When she opened them again she saw one couple rising to their feet. They paid and fled. Neen winced. She doubted they'd ever return.

Travis's mother eyed the till greedily. 'I'll have your wages, boy! You sponge off me like some parasite and I'll have what's owing to me.'

The final customer shot to her feet, threw some money down and left. Joey hid beneath his table. Neen saw him crouching there, his eyes wide in his pale face, and her heart lurched. She knew exactly how he felt—terrorised—and it made her want to weep.

She turned back to the interloper and swallowed. 'Hello, Mrs Cooper. I'm pleased to meet you.' She kept her voice calm and reasonable. She didn't want any trouble. She didn't want Joey more frightened than he already was. 'I'm Neen—Travis's boss.'

The café door opened and a customer entered. Neen didn't glance up. She kept her eyes on the woman opposite in case one of her self-defence moves was needed.

'I know who you are, and I ain't here to see you. I'm here to talk to my boy.'

Joey tried to curl himself up into as small a ball as possible. Travis's face darkened and both his hands clenched to fists. Neen swallowed back the torrent of angry words clawing at her throat. Yelling and ranting at a drunken woman would do no good.

Reaching into the till, she extracted a twenty-dollar note. 'If I give you this, will you just turn around and walk out of here?'

Mrs Cooper eyed the money and licked her lips.

The customer by the door let the door swing shut and started towards them with a speed that had Neen stepping back, heart in her mouth. But as she glanced up her shoulders sagged. *Rico*. She wasn't sure she'd ever been so pleased to see anyone in her life.

He reached across and plucked the money from Neen's fingers. 'You'll do no such thing!' His glare almost singed her on the spot.

'Oy!' Mrs Cooper yelled.

He turned to her, his eyes hard and cold. 'How much have you had to drink?'

'None of your business,' she slurred, shaping up to him.

'If you don't turn around and leave now, I will call the police.'

Neen barely recognised this cold, hard stranger masquerading as Rico. She swallowed and glanced again at Joey, still curled up into a ball. At Travis, whose face had gone from an unhealthy grey to a dark, foreboding red.

Mrs Cooper swayed. 'You don't frighten me!'

Rico pulled his cell phone from his pocket.

'Ah, you and your hoity-toity ways,' she hollered. 'Fine, fine! I'm going. See?'

He walked to the door and held it open with pointed emphasis. She stormed out of it. Rico slammed it shut, locked it, and turned the sign to 'Closed'. Then he swung to her. 'What the hell—?'

She shook her head as Travis let fly with a word that made her ears burn. He moved as if to punch the back wall, but she launched herself at him, grabbing his hand and hauling him to a chair. He swore again, slammed a fist down on the table.

'Take a deep breath,' she ordered, her hands on his shoulders—partly for comfort, but partly to keep him in his seat. He dragged in a great hulking breath, but she didn't release him. Anger still rippled through him at too great a rate. 'And another.'

She met Rico's gaze and hitched her head to where Joey still hid beneath the table.

It didn't take him long to cajole Joey out. She waited for him to hug the boy and offer him comfort. When he didn't, she opened one arm and Joey flew to her side.

When she finally felt the tension ease out of Travis, she relaxed her hold on him. 'I want you to know that whatever your mother does won't reflect on you. You're doing a great job here and I'm proud of you. I don't want you to forget that, okay?'

He pulled in another breath and gave a short nod. Then he grimaced. 'Sorry I swore. I…I thought she was going to ruin everything for Joey and me.'

'Not a chance,' she managed, the pounding of her heart starting to slow.

'Travis,' Joey whispered, 'can we sleep in the shed again tonight?'

What? 'Not a chance,' she said. 'You two are coming home with me this evening.' She winked at Joey. 'Do you like dogs?'

He nodded.

'I have a huge doofus of a dog who's going to *love* you.'

'Really?'

'Really,' she assured him, wincing at the mayhem she could imagine boy and dog creating.

'I…uh…' Travis cleared his throat and stared at her. 'But…'

She sent him a reassuring smile. 'It's not a problem, honest. I'll welcome the company.'

The relief on his face was the only thanks she needed. He swallowed. 'I…uh…haven't finished cleaning the kitchen.'

'Well, you go get the kitchen sorted while I clear up the last bits and pieces out here.'

He went, taking Joey with him. Only then did she meet Rico's silent gaze.

In two strides he was right in front of her, bristling, invading her space. 'What do you think you were doing, offering money to an alcoholic?'

From all that had just happened, *that* was the thread he wanted to pick up?

Those cold, hard eyes bored into hers. 'Don't you realise how irresponsible that was?'

She wanted to step back, but she refused to show such weakness. 'I wanted to get rid of her as quickly as possible, with the minimum of fuss.' For Joey's sake. And Travis's.

'And what did you plan to do when she turned up tomorrow, spouting the same rubbish and expecting the same handout? What were you going to do when her friends caught wind of it and started showing up?'

She swallowed. She hadn't been thinking that far ahead.

He slashed a hand through the air. 'You cannot reason with an alcoholic or a drug addict.'

'I…I'm sorry. It won't happen again.'

'It had better not!'

His tone chilled her to her marrow.

He thrust a finger under her nose, his lips twisting. 'And let's get another thing straight while we're at it, so there are no further misunderstandings. If there's the slightest hint of alcohol or drug abuse among any of the boys, I want to know. Not tomorrow. Not next week. But immediately. You hear me?'

'Yes.'

She forced herself to hold his gaze. It was angry,

bitter…disgusted. She took a step back, her heart hammering.

'Do you always take the path of least resistance?' His lip curled. 'Is that what you did with Chris?'

All the frustration she'd held back for Joey and Travis's sakes clamoured through her now. 'So now you're going to start using Chris as a weapon against me? Well, I've got news for you.' She lifted her chin and set her feet. 'I will *not* be bullied like that again.'

He swung away. 'I'm not bullying you!'

'Then what would you call it?'

He stilled and then turned back. The disgust in his eyes drained away and it suddenly occurred to her that it had never been aimed at her in the first place. 'I…' He rubbed his neck. 'Sorry.'

She nodded and chafed her arms.

'One last thing before we're done.'

Brilliant.

'You are *not* taking Travis and Joey home for the night.'

'You're right.' She let the hard ball of anger in her stomach grow and spread throughout her entire body until she hummed with it. 'They're not staying for a night, but probably a whole week.'

He opened his mouth.

'And unless you want an all-out mutiny on your hands you'll shut your mouth, turn around and walk out—*now*.'

CHAPTER EIGHT

'THEY'VE BEEN LIVING with you for over a week, Neen. It has to stop!'

'I thought I was here to discuss the gala event, not my living arrangements.'

Rico's hands clenched. 'I'm responsible for—'

'The success of the café. Nothing more.'

Her pigheaded refusal to see sense made his shoulders and back tighten up until they almost cramped. Whisking her away to his office for the final two hours of the day to discuss preparations for the Melbourne Cup luncheon had simply been a pretext to get her alone, to discuss Travis and Joey's situation without the possibility of them overhearing.

He slammed a hand down on his desk. 'I'm responsible for this situation. I'm responsible for the welfare of those boys.'

The fire in her eyes made his mouth dry. 'Are you insinuating that Travis and Joey are in danger from me?'

'Don't be ridiculous.'

She stabbed a finger at him. 'You *know* they're

physically, mentally and morally better off with me than they are with their mother. So what is your problem?'

'The problem is you're not their legal guardian!' Couldn't she see she was opening herself up for all kinds of legal complications if anything went wrong? She had enough trouble in her life without adding this to the tally.

The café would be toast too, if the press ever got hold of this kind of story. Their hard work would be for nothing!

'In a couple more weeks Travis comes of age. He means to petition for legal guardianship of Joey and apply for public-funded housing. Do you doubt he'll be granted either one of those things?'

'No.'

'Two weeks. That's all I'm asking for, Rico.'

It wasn't that simple. 'If someone reports you…' He let the sentence hang, hoping it would give her a moment's pause.

'The only person who would do that, Rico, is you. As long as their mother continues to receive her child allowance she'll stay quiet.'

That, at least, was true.

'*Are* you going to report me?'

He *should* report it. There were processes and procedures in place to keep everyone safe in a situation like this. Bypassing them was foolhardy. 'Look, Neen, it means Joey goes into foster care for less than month. He'll be fed, clothed and housed. It's not like it's the end of the world. Travis can visit him.'

'But they won't be together, and you know that's what matters to them most! And haven't they been through enough?'

She burst out of her chair, paced to the far wall and then back to his desk. She planted her hands on the surface and leaned across it, eyes flashing.

And just like that the blood in Rico's veins blazed fierce and hot. A pulse of need pounded through him as he stared at her. He tried to force his mind back to the discussion but all he could focus on was the sweet swell of Neen's mouth, the vivid blue of her eyes and the smooth, creamy skin of her neck.

'What if Travis does a runner with Joey? Have you considered that?'

That snapped him back. 'Is there any danger of that?'

She fell into her chair, shoulders slumping, and bile filled his mouth.

'I think the only thing that keeps Travis going most days is caring for Joey. He's had a glimpse of a brighter future and he's holding fast to it.' She gave a short laugh. 'It's not an easy future by any means, but it's a brighter one, and…'

Those amazing eyes of hers turned to freezing chips of ice.

'And if you kick the chair out from underneath him, if you take that vision away from him, Rico, if you even make it harder to reach, then…'

She swallowed and folded her arms—but not before he noticed the way her hands shook.

'Then you'll be doing him a grave disservice. You'll be doing us *all* a grave disservice.'

He was trying to make a difference! A positive difference to keep them all safe. And yet—

She leaned towards him. He couldn't name the expression in her eyes. It wasn't disappointment. He'd learned early on to recognise that emotion in his mother's face. But it was closely akin.

'When did the cause become more important than the individual?' she demanded.

He remained silent.

'You people with your causes and so-called good works! You don't care who you trample in the process of achieving what you want, do you?'

That was when he finally recognised the expression in her eyes—hurt. 'Neen.' Her name croaked out of him. 'I'm not trying to hurt you.' He was trying to *protect* her!

'No? Well, you are.' Her chin came up and she gave another one of those short, harsh laughs that scraped across each and every one of his nerves. 'But don't worry. I have enough experience with these things to know how it goes. I know it doesn't make a scrap of difference how I feel, because in the end it simply won't make a scrap of difference to your decision. I'll just be another victim of friendly fire, right?'

He shot to his feet. 'What are you talking about?

I'm trying to stop you from getting into a situation that could cause you a lot of trouble and grief.' He reefed a hand back through his hair. 'You can't get personally involved in these boys' lives. It's the first rule in the book.'

'Whose book?' she snapped. 'Yours? Is that why you wouldn't give a little kid a hug when he needed it? Because your rotten rulebook says you're not to get involved? That's no way to lead your life, and I'm sure as heck not going to follow stupid advice like that.'

'It's not stupid. It's the smart thing to do.'

'Smart for who?'

'For everyone!'

'I'm sorry, Rico, but I refuse to live the kind of half-life you do. When I wake up in the morning I want to be able to look at myself in the mirror without flinching.'

Everything inside him went cold. 'This is not the way to save the world.'

'I'm not the least bit interested in saving the world. I just want to help Travis and Joey.'

They stared at each. Both breathed hard.

'Rico, I have the right to choose what battles I fight. And I think this battle is one worth fighting for. I'm prepared to accept the consequences, if there are any.'

For a moment the room spun.

'I understand you want to protect your asset.'

He sat, frowned. 'Asset?'

'That's what I am, isn't it?' Her voice remained matter-of-fact—hard, even—but her eyes didn't, and the accusation in them burned his soul. 'I'm an asset to your café, to your cause.'

He saw himself through her eyes and loathed what he saw. He recalled the way she'd held Joey close to her side, the way her hand had curved into Travis's shoulder, and had to close his eyes.

'But I will tell you this, Rico.'

He forced his eyes open again.

'If you interfere with the arrangement I have with Travis and Joey, I'll resign.'

'You signed a contract!'

'So sue me. Your choice.'

Choice? He pressed a thumb and forefinger to his eyes. He'd run out of choices ten years ago.

That's not Neen's fault.

He lifted his head. 'What did you mean about having experience? Experience of what?' People like him—driven, following the rulebook to get things done in the most efficient and safest way possible? His hand clenched. It *did* get things done.

Her gaze slipped from his. 'Does it matter?'

'It might have a bearing on how I proceed.'

That was a blatant lie. But if he knew more about her it might give him a clue as to how to talk her out of the course of action she was so determined to take. He couldn't report Travis and Joey. Not if it meant losing Neen. His heart sank to his knees. And he certainly couldn't take that course of action if it meant Travis would do a runner. That kid had a bright future and Rico didn't want to jeopardise it. Neen was right on one score—Travis had been through enough.

But not reporting them meant throwing the rule-book out of the window.

Still, he knew Travis and Joey would thrive at Neen's…

'My parents—' She moistened her lips, but she didn't look at him. 'They run a dog shelter.'

He shrugged. What was so bad about that? Sure, she professed to hate dogs, but her manner with Monty debunked that claim.

'All my life I've come second to those darn dogs.' She gave him a tight, bitter smile. 'Oh, I know that sounds like a bad case of sour grapes, but…'

But she wasn't the kind of person to hold a grudge.

'If it wasn't for my grandfather, who came to live with us when he learned of the situation, there'd have been nights when I wouldn't have eaten and days when I wouldn't have made it to school.'

His eyes narrowed. 'Why not?'

'Because my parents were too busy racing off to save some dog from one vile situation or another.'

He stiffened. His nostrils flared, though he tried to stop them.

She must have seen the condemnation in his eyes—condemnation aimed squarely at her parents—because she shrugged and added, 'To be fair, they knew my grandfather would pick up the slack.'

It didn't change the fact that her parents hadn't fulfilled their duty of care towards her. He recalled seeing a photograph of them at Neen's. They'd looked so normal and mild. He'd long ago learned, however, that appearances could be deceptive.

Her lips twisted. 'What made things interesting for a while was my utter fear of dogs. But they still forced me to help clean the cages and exercise them.'

He scraped a hand down his face. He'd seen first-hand what that kind of fear could do to a kid. Neen's resilience filled him with a new respect for her. And admiration.

She smoothed her hair back behind her ears. 'Lots and lots of people had it far worse than I ever did. You must hear their stories every day.'

Those stories, however, never became easier to hear, and every day they made him sick to the stomach. Sick with helplessness and guilt. Guilt that he couldn't do more. Guilt that he'd been one of the lucky ones when he'd done nothing to deserve it. And fear—a constant nagging fear followed him everywhere. Fear that other kids would make the same mistakes he had and pay the price for it. A price that was too high.

'I wasn't beaten or starved or left without a roof over my head.'

But she had been neglected. He could see now why she'd fallen for a control freak like Chris.

'My parents made it clear that those dogs had no-

body else to rely on for their survival but them, nobody else to rescue them from appalling situations.'

'That's not true. There's the RSPCA, and any
number of other animal welfare agencies.'

She nodded. 'It doesn't change the fact that
they've done a lot of good.'

Yet it was Neen who'd been forced to make the
sacrifices.

'To be perfectly honest, a different kid might
have thrived in those conditions. There were kids
at school who envied me. I was always encouraged
to bring those kids home to "help out". The shelter
was always short of volunteers.'

He winced. 'That was just downright selfish of
them.'

'Ah, but selfish for a *good cause*.'

Was that how she saw him? He lifted his head.
Was he like that?

She shrugged. 'I always understood that if I
wanted to go on to further study I would have to
pay for it myself, which was fair enough. It was
their money, and what they chose to do with it was
their affair.'

He couldn't be quite so blasé about it.

'But, Rico, they went a step too far when they decided to contest my grandfather's will.'

His jaw dropped. He had no hope of keeping the
shock from his face. He leaned towards her. 'It's
your *parents* who are contesting the will?'

The lift of her chin and the set of her lips did nothing to hide the pain in the deep blue of her eyes. 'I've offered them a percentage of the will, but they've refused. They believe they're entitled to the entire amount.'

He couldn't think of a single thing to say. Other than swear words, that was, but he knew her opinion of those.

'They obviously believe their dream is more important than mine, but this time I'm fighting back. Because... Because Grandad did so much—not just for me but for them too—and this shows me they didn't value it at all—' She broke off and gripped her hands together. 'They didn't even attend his funeral. They were too busy off somewhere saving some mutt or other. He deserved better!' She stared down at her hands. Eventually she lifted her gaze. 'His final wishes mean nothing to them.'

Whereas they meant the world to his granddaughter.

'They trampled all over him in life, taking him for granted. I'm not going to let them do that to him in death.'

I have the right to choose my battles.

'So...' She smoothed her hair back again. 'Has my nasty little story made a difference to how you mean to deal with Travis and Joey?'

Yes! A thousand times, *yes*. He wasn't going to turn a blind eye to the situation. Not a chance of that. He'd do whatever he could to actively help.

But...

He lifted his chin. 'You think I'm like your parents?'

'In some regards.' She stared back at him. 'But they like what they do. In fact, they love it. They wouldn't want to be doing anything else. You don't love your job. For some reason, though, you're just as driven as they are. Like them, you define yourself by what you do. You're more than just your job, Rico, but you refuse to see it.'

'You think I hurt people for the greater good?' He could see she didn't want to answer that. 'Neen?'

'Well, *don't* you?'

He opened his mouth. Closed it again. His stomach churned so badly it took all of his strength to stop it from rebelling completely.

'Toeing the line is very important to you,' she said.

Because it protected everyone. It was the safe way of getting things done. He'd started to see, though, that it might not always be the kindest way. 'If I don't follow rules, Neen, my funding gets cut.' And if his funding got cut that meant fewer boys could get off the streets and keep safe.

'It's why you don't get personally involved, isn't it? It's the reason you don't befriend the boys. Because if you did maybe you wouldn't be able to stop yourself from bending the rules once in a blue moon when the situation called for it.'

Her words struck at the core of him. 'Neen, I—'

'Do you know you speak to the boys the same way your mother speaks to you?'

He stiffened. 'I do *not*!'

She stared at him for a long moment. 'I take it that's not how you mean to come across?'

Heck, no! He raked a hand through his hair. Did he really come across as that angry and bitter?

'I understand you being passionate about your work, but…'

He wanted to sleep for a hundred years. He pressed a thumb and forefinger to his eyes. 'But?'

'Doing your job kindly, with a smile and with friendliness…that wouldn't detract from what you're doing, would it?'

How could he tell her that if he relaxed, let his guard down for a moment and remembered what it was like to feel alive and have fun, he was afraid he'd turn his back on this job and never return?

And how could he do that to Louis?

He'd thought that as time went on this job would get easier, but it only became harder—demanded more and more from him.

'I'm sorry. I don't mean to come across so churlish and bad-tempered. Not to anyone.'

She didn't say anything, and finally he lifted his head to meet her gaze. Her eyes had softened. A man could drown in that particular shade of blue.

'I kinda guessed that.'

He would need to find another reserve of energy for smiles and pleasantries, for being friendly and remembering who supported which football team and whatnot…for patience.

'The sixty-four-thousand-dollar question, though, is why you *do*.'

For a moment he was tempted to spread the whole sorry tale on the table for her—he ached to do just that—but he already knew the outcome. Neen would absolve him, and that wasn't an outcome he deserved.

'Because I'm a jerk?'

She glanced away, and he knew she'd recognised his evasion for what it was.

'You know, sometimes I think you're my friend.' She glanced back and folded her arms. 'Every now and again I think I glimpse more in you than the driven do-gooder too busy to chat to someone who's feeling down. I made the mistake of thinking you saw me as more than just a means to an end. I made the mistake of thinking you saw me as a friend too.'

That was when he realised how much he'd hurt her on a personal level. He remembered that kiss and—

Bile burned his stomach. Acid burned his throat. 'There are things you don't know about me.'

'Like what?' she challenged. 'Go on—why not share?' she drawled, in a voice that told him she didn't expect him to. 'Hey, my life's practically an open book to you now. There's nothing else to know.'

Nonsense! There was the shape of her body beneath his hands and—

He clenched his jaw and wrenched his gaze away. Maybe it would be better if she *did* know the truth.

Once she did she'd never have unrealistic expectations about him again. That would make for a better relationship in the long run.

He glanced back and his attention snagged on the shape of her mouth. He dragged it back to the matter in hand. A *working* relationship was all he was interested in. If she tried to offer him comfort and absolution, he wouldn't accept it. He knew what he was due, and the debts were still outstanding.

'When I was a teenager...' The words scraped out of his throat. 'I became involved in drugs. There was absolutely no excuse for it. I came from a good home, but...'

She blinked and her eyes became the colour of the sky at twilight. 'Oh, Rico.'

The words were nothing more than a breath, but he had to steel himself against them. 'When I was seventeen I bought drugs from a dealer I'd never met before—bought them with money stolen from my mother's purse.'

She winced, but whether from the picture he'd painted or his harsh tone he couldn't tell.

'The heroin was too pure and my best friend overdosed on it. He died and it was my fault.'

Raw pain stretched through his words, darkening his face and twisting it, and it all fell into place—the reason why he drove himself so hard.

She wanted to wrap her arms around him and

offer him the same comfort she had Joey and Travis a week ago, only she knew he'd refuse it.

She could see from the self-loathing deep in his eyes that he didn't believe he'd been punished enough. Not yet. Probably never.

She fought the urge to drop her head to the desk and weep for him. 'How long ago was that, Rico? Nine or ten years? Don't you think you've repaid your debt to society?'

He reared back and his pallor made her stomach lurch.

'Repaid my debt?' He shoved his chair back. 'Louis died. He *died*! Nothing I do—*nothing*—will ever bring him back.'

She swallowed and nodded. 'You're right. So don't you think it's time you stopped trying to?'

He shook his head. 'I'm to blame for his death. *Me!*' His eyes glittered. 'And, no, I can't bring him back. But I can make sure he didn't die in vain. I can do everything I can to prevent teenagers from making the same mistakes we did.'

Her mouth dried. 'It could've just as easily been you who died that night, Rico.'

'A fact that still gives my mother nightmares.'

She had to close her eyes, just for a moment. 'I think you're wrong. I think it's time you forgave yourself.' She opened her eyes wide to glare at him. 'Would Louis hold you responsible like this? Would you want him blaming himself like this if your situations were reversed?'

He stared back, his eyes cold, hard, dark. But it was all aimed inwards, not at her.

'You weren't there. You didn't see him die that ugly death. You didn't see the expression in his parents' eyes when they looked at me.'

She sucked in a breath and then leaped to her feet. 'You were younger than Travis is now! If something like that happened to *him* you'd pull out all the stops to help him, to get him the support he needed, the counselling.'

He said nothing. Just stared back at her with hooded eyes.

'I can't imagine you'd encourage him to immolate himself on a pyre of self-sacrifice.'

'I had chances Travis never had.'

'That doesn't mean there weren't reasons for why you went off the rails like you did. Your family had such high expectations of you. That kind of pressure is hard to cope with. Not to mention unfair.'

'Oh, poor me,' he mocked.

She ignored that. 'And you lost your father when you were fifteen! You'd have been grieving and angry.' Who could've blamed him for that? 'I've met your mother, your brothers, Rico.' The picture grew clearer in her mind. 'They probably threw themselves into work in an effort to deal with their grief and refused to let you join them. Not because they were trying to exclude you, but because as far as they were concerned you were meant for better things. I bet you felt excluded.'

She swung away to pace the length of the office.

'They were trying to live their dreams through you—which was patently unfair, I might add—and they gave you no chance for an outlet.' She swung back. 'No wonder you went off the rails.'

'There's no excuse for what I did.'

He'd made a mistake and he was paying such a high price for it. She brushed away a tear, knowing he wouldn't want to see it.

'What there's no excuse for, Rico, is you not grabbing your second chance with both hands and living the life you should be living. You seem to think you have no right to happiness or enjoyment—even for half an hour. You seem to think the only way you can do good is in this job of yours. Imagine how much more good you could do if you were doing a job you loved?'

'I am doing good right where I am. I am making a difference.'

But in the process he was hurting himself, and although he couldn't have explained it to her, that somehow cancelled out some of the good he did.

'But—'

'I don't want to hear it, Neen.' He lifted his chin. 'But now you know.'

She stared at him. She ached to bring back the man who'd worked side by side with her during that rush hour at the café. The man who'd come alive. The man who'd glowed with zest and passion.

But Rico was intent on burying that man.

Whether he was aware of it or not, though, the cracks were starting to show. His horror when she'd pointed out to him how he spoke to the boys being a case in point. Rico might be intent on keeping his heart under house arrest, but she was suddenly determined to keep chipping away at those walls. Rico deserved so much more than this life he'd chained himself to.

'Rico—'

He held up a hand and pressed a button on his intercom. 'Lisle, could you order a prepaid cab to take Ms Cuthbert back to the café, please?' He began assembling files on his desk. 'The cab should be here any moment.' He didn't look up.

Without a word, Neen rose and left his office.

'I spy, with my little eye, something beginning with *W*.'

The doorbell rang and Neen gave up a silent prayer of thanks. It was Monday and Joey was not long home from school. She'd discovered that while he was quiet at the café, he more than made up for it at home.

Still, she didn't let that make her careless. She glanced through the peephole.

She took a step back, her heart thumping like a mad thing. She smoothed down her shirt, tucked her hair behind her ears and then peeped again. Shaking herself, she opened the door.

'Rico—hello.' He'd been a virtual stranger since their conversation in his office last week.

'Neen.' He nodded his greeting. 'I hope you don't mind that I've dropped around like this. I'm not trying to hijack your weekend or anything.'

She almost smiled at that. 'Not at all. Come on in.'

He didn't move. 'I just wanted to give you this.' He pulled an envelope from his jacket pocket and held it out to her.

She didn't look at it. She looked at him. 'Rico.' She folded her arms. 'You're here now. The least you can do is come in for a cuppa.' She knew the way he skipped meals and whatnot. He was probably in dire need of some sustenance.

He hesitated.

'I'd really welcome some adult company.' It wasn't a plea—not precisely.

His lips twitched.

'Who is it, Neen?' Joey glanced around her and immediately went quiet.

'It's Rico. He's coming in for a cup of tea. Would you like to put the tea leaves in the pot like I showed you?'

His face lit up and he raced off to find the teapot.

Rico wavered for a moment. 'Maybe just a quick cuppa.' He finally stepped over the threshold, closing the door behind him.

He stood close to her, and she could feel both the cool of the spring day on his clothes and the heat from his body. It was strangely intoxicating.

'Is he frightened of me?' he asked in a low voice.

She snapped back. 'You intimidate him,' she murmured.

'I don't want to intimidate people.'

No, he wanted to help them. In fact, Rico wanted to save the world. 'Then I suggest you try smiling at him without the weight of the world in your eyes… and maybe talk about cricket.'

Neen didn't live too far from the Bellerive cricket oval—Tasmania's and one of Australia's prime cricket grounds. This fact delighted Joey to bits as he was planning on becoming the next Australian cricket captain.

'Cricket?' Rico smiled suddenly. 'I used to be pretty good at schoolboy cricket.'

She wondered when he'd last taken the time to watch a game.

He followed her into the kitchen and glanced around. 'Where's Travis?'

'I sent him into town to watch a movie with some friends.'

Joey showed her the teapot. 'I put three teaspoons in.'

'That's perfect, Joey.'

He beamed at her, cast a glance at Rico and sidled off to wrestle with Monty in the living room. He and Monty had become firm friends.

Only after the tea had brewed and she'd poured out two mugs and set out some choc-chip cookies did Neen finally look Rico full in the face and hold out her hand. 'You had something for me?'

He reached into his pocket again and handed her the envelope he'd proffered earlier. Her stomach clenched. Would it be some kind of summons demanding that Joey leave for a foster home or—?

She swallowed and broke open the seal, read the enclosed document.

She reread it.

Three times.

She glanced at the man opposite, a lump in her throat the size of a cricket ball. She tried to swallow it. 'This…this is a form assigning me as Joey's foster parent.'

He didn't say anything.

'And it has his mother's blessing.'

He drank tea and ate a cookie.

'Rico!' She shook his arm, unable to hide the grin that built through her. 'How did you *do* this?'

'I had a quiet word with the boys' mother and she came to see that this was the best solution for the moment.'

Her mouth opened and closed. 'I…I know you don't approve of what I'm doing—'

'It's not that I don't approve. I just don't want you in a position that could compromise you or where you could be sued.'

He was doing what he always did. 'Thank you.' She held the document to her chest. 'I mean that from the bottom of my heart, Rico. Thank you.'

'It's only a temporary measure,' he warned. 'Mrs Cooper has agreed to go into an alcohol rehabilitation programme. So...' He shrugged.

'Fingers crossed,' she murmured, and then she swallowed. 'I really didn't mean for my actions to reflect badly on your project.'

His head shot up. 'Do you think *that's* what this is about?'

She stared at him for a long moment. She reached out and seized her mug. 'You'd better be careful, Rico, because if the answer to that is no then you might find yourself breaking your rules and getting personally involved.' But she smiled as she said it.

He scowled, and she had to bite back a laugh. Before either one of them could respond, a tennis ball clattered across the table, upsetting Rico's cup and sending the cookies flying.

'Joey!' she hollered.

He appeared in the doorway, biting his lip. 'Sorry, Neen.'

With a sigh, she set about mopping up the mess.

'Neen tells me you like cricket,' said Rico.

From the corner of her eye she watched as Joey took a step into the room. 'Uh-huh.' He nodded, his expression wary, but she could see he was aching to be won over.

'Do you play in your team at school?'

Rico wasn't a natural, but he was trying. She had to give him that.

'Uh-huh,' Joey repeated.

Rico patted the chair beside him. 'What position do you play? I used to be an opening batsman for my school team.'

Joey was up on the chair in a flash. 'I'm wicketkeeper, because Mr Reynolds says I have a good eye. But what I really want to do is hit sixes.'

'There's no reason why you can't be a wicketkeeper who hits sixes,' Rico said, and the young boy's eyes went wide at a possibility he evidently hadn't considered.

Monty chose that moment to drop a ball into Rico's lap.

'It's time for his walk,' Joey said. 'You wanna come too?'

Neen found herself holding her breath as she waited for his reply.

Joey stared up at Rico hopefully. 'We can take my cricket bat.'

Rico suddenly smiled, and Neen's heart did a dance. 'How can I turn down an offer like that?'

She promptly collected Monty's lead and hustled them all outside and in the direction of the beach. Joey and Monty raced ahead. Rico carried the cricket bat. And Neen carried a heart lighter than it had any right to be.

'Is he running you ragged?'

'Completely.'

He gave a soft laugh. 'And you're loving every moment of it.'

She loved him for not telling her there were other

options, that she could hand this problem over to someone else, someone more qualified.

She cleared her throat. No, not *loved*. She liked—appreciated—that he didn't try to change her mind on the matter. She liked it a lot.

She shook her head, feeling freer than she had since before her grandad had died. 'Who'd have thought it, huh? Who'd have thought I'd enjoy that rotten dog, or your rotten café, or a seven-year-old boy? A miracle—that's what this is.'

'One of your own making.'

They reached the strip of beach. She thought back to the document sitting on her kitchen table and shook her head. Rico was the miracle worker.

CHAPTER NINE

THEY PLAYED A vigorous game of beach cricket—she, Joey, Monty and Rico.

Even in his suit trousers and business shirt Rico breathed athleticism, and it shouldn't have surprised her but it did. She couldn't drag her gaze from him. When he was charging through life, his mind focused on his next meeting, his next funding application, preoccupied with the outcome of the previous one, it was easy to ignore him.

She scratched her nose. Well, it was easier. Rico was impossible to ignore in any of his guises. But he was irresistible when he played beach cricket.

He was irresistible when he cooked too, but his body wasn't on such blatant display then. The breadth of his shoulders and the powerful musculature of his thighs made an ache start up deep inside.

It didn't help that he smiled a lot either.

Some of the smiles weren't wholly genuine. *I don't mean to be intimidating.* But some of them were, and the more he did it the easier it seemed to become for him. Each and every one of them made her heart catch. Not to mention her breath.

He wasn't wholly at ease one hundred per cent of the time with Joey either. But he was making an effort and, like a lot of seven-year-olds, Joey forgave him the gaps and the occasional awkwardness. But when Rico and Joey talked cricket and Rico showed Joey different ways to grip the cricket bat, they were so focused they could have been the only two people on the beach.

Rico, to her utter delight, wore out both Joey and Monty completely. 'Dinnertime,' she finally announced, pointing at her watch.

Rico glanced at his own watch and his eyes widened. He jogged over to where she sat and offered her his hand. With a little thrill she took it and he hauled her to her feet. She slid in the sand. It shifted her closer to him and she had to reach out and steady herself against his arm.

Beneath her fingers, his biceps were warm and firm. He smelled of salt and sweat and aftershave. Her fingers curled into his shirt. He held her hand a beat too long and her heart surged against her ribs. She glanced up at him. Hunger flared in his eyes… but then the shutters slammed down over his face.

She pulled away at the same time that he released her. She smoothed a hand down over her shirt and did what she could to get her wayward pulse under control. 'I think you should play hooky more often.'

She cleared her throat and pasted on a smile. 'It's good for you.'

That darkness at the back of his eyes stirred.

She pushed a strand of hair behind her ears. 'It's certainly good for me.' She nodded towards Joey and Monty. 'The rest of my evening is now going to be much more peaceful.'

Finally his lips hooked up. 'I had fun.' He reached out and ruffled Joey's hair. 'And when Joey here makes the Australian team I can say I knew him way back when.'

She mentally reached for a hammer and chisel. 'Well, the least we can do is make you dinner.' She was careful to keep her voice on the neutral side of friendly.

He didn't answer, but she sensed his withdrawal. She chafed her arms.

'What are we having, Neen? I'm starved.'

'Fish done in a yummy sauce, salad…and a potato salad if we can talk Rico into making it for us.'

Happy with that, Joey clipped on Monty's lead and ran off ahead with him while she and Rico followed at a more leisurely pace.

'I know it's short notice, and I understand if you have other plans, but you're more than welcome to join us.' She glanced at him from the corner of her eye and held her breath. 'I wouldn't mind having a bit of a chat about the café too. We never quite got to it during our meeting on Friday.' She lifted one

shoulder. 'Of course if you'd rather slot that in for
another time during the week, we can do that.'

'It's your day off, Neen.'

He spoke quietly. She swung to him, hands on
hips. 'When on earth has that ever mattered to *you*,
Mr Workaholic? I'd thought you'd be happy with
this proof of my commitment.'

'Your commitment isn't in doubt.'

She raised an eyebrow.

'Anymore,' he amended.

For reasons she couldn't begin to explain, that
made her smile. She dragged in a breath of salt air
and shivered a little. It might be spring, but with
the sun almost sunk beneath the horizon the night
air was chilly.

He frowned. 'Cold?'

He'd left his jacket hanging over one of her kitchen
chairs, and she could see him mentally berate himself for that. The thought of him settling his jacket
over her shoulders made her shiver again, but this
time not with the cold.

'My fault. I should've thought to bring a sweater.
But it's no problem because we're home now.'

Rico followed her into the house without hesitation. When he didn't shrug immediately into his
jacket she decided to interpret that as one more for
dinner.

Joey and Monty planted themselves in front of the
television. 'Rico!' Joey called out. 'Next time you

come to play I think you should wear a tracksuit. You'll be able to play cricket better then.'

Neen choked back a laugh. 'Excellent suggestion, Joey,' she agreed, tossing Rico an apron.

'Out of the mouths of babes…' Rico muttered.

'Do you even own a tracksuit?'

He glared. 'Of course I do.'

She retrieved potatoes from the pantry. 'I was starting to think you even slept in your suits.'

'I sleep naked, Neen.'

She promptly dropped a potato. Rico caught it before it hit the floor. She sent the rest tumbling across the bench. Rico naked? Her mouth dried. Rico naked…

Oh, bad thought. *Bad* thought! *Stop it!*

He grinned and winked, as if he sensed the heat that had careened through her. It was only the tiniest glimpse of the fun, sexy Rico, but it sent her pulse twitching and dancing. It suddenly occurred to her that chipping away at Rico might prove a little dangerous.

It wasn't a thought designed to settle her pulse.

'Nice catch,' she managed, her voice husky.

His gaze settled on her lips and his eyes turned dark and smoky. Time stilled and any hope of catching her breath fled.

Neen shook herself and stepped back, her pulse thundering in her ears. She wasn't getting cosy with Rico. Besides the fact he was her boss, and getting involved with one's boss was never a clever move, he was too driven. She'd forever come a poor second to his work.

She lifted her chin. She deserved better than that.

When she was ready to dip her toes in romantic waters again, that was.

And that time wasn't yet.

But it hit her that when they'd walked down to the beach earlier she hadn't once scanned the neighbourhood—the sidewalks, roads and the park—for signs of anything amiss…for signs of Chris. She swallowed. In fact she hadn't thought about Chris once. Rico made her feel safe.

What? So you're just going to latch onto him?

She stiffened. No way! Friends. That was all.

She seized a potato and held it up. 'Listen carefully and learn the art of making the perfect potato salad.'

She had to close her eyes when he gave her his full attention.

Dinner should have been pleasant. Normally she enjoyed Joey's chatter. This afternoon she'd enjoyed watching Rico and Joey interact. But behind all the pleasant banter and good food was a dark thrumming in her blood that gave her no peace.

'I'll do the dishes while you get Joey ready for bed,' Rico offered when the meal was finished.

'Deal.'

Before she could usher Joey towards the bathroom to brush his teeth, he swung to Rico. 'Thank you for teaching me more about cricket. I really liked it a lot.'

'You're welcome.'

They both stood there awkwardly for a moment, and then Joey surged forward and flung his arms around Rico's middle.

Rico blinked, but his arms went around the boy. He kind of clumsily but kind of nicely patted the young boy's back. 'Sleep well, Joey.'

Neen left him blinking and dazed, her own chest tight and constricted.

The dishes were practically done when she returned. He glanced at her, and then back at the dish he was wiping. 'I forget to say earlier, but thank you for dinner. I enjoyed it.'

'So did Joey.' She set about putting the clean crockery away. 'Besides, you helped.'

He huffed out a sigh. 'I enjoyed that too.'

She turned from the cupboard. 'There's no shame in that, Rico. Louis is dead and you can't bring him back. You are working at making a difference in the world. And you *are* making a difference. You're allowed to let your hair down and enjoy yourself occasionally. In fact, I think you should be proud of the way you've turned your life around and of all you've accomplished.'

His head reared back.

She refused to give the darkness time to claim him. 'Joey's a good kid, isn't he?'

He seemed to fight with himself for a moment, but then he nodded. 'Yeah, he really is.'

'You did good work today, playing with him like you did and talking about cricket. He has a lot of energy.' Energy that could get him into trouble later on. 'You've helped give him a place to channel that energy.' She filled the jug and set it to boil. 'You've made me realise where I can help him channel that energy too.'

He turned to her, suddenly serious. 'You know this situation is only temporary? Travis and Joey will only be here for another couple of weeks.'

She stilled, and then she grinned and clapped her hands. 'You have housing already lined up for Travis, don't you?'

'I'm working on it.'

She should have known.

'Look, I know it's only temporary, but if you think I'm giving up my honorary aunt status, you have another think coming. Travis will need support, not to mention the occasional babysitter.'

His eyes widened. He leaned towards her. 'But…'

She waited, but he didn't continue. She busied herself making coffee. She turned back and handed him a mug.

'We've become friends, Rico. It happens in lots of workplaces.' She motioned to the freshly cleaned and cleared kitchen table. She sensed his mind racing behind the dark sparkle of his eyes.

'You've had more of a positive impact on Travis and Joey's lives than I ever have,' he said.

She couldn't tell if that bothered him or not. She sat down. 'On a personal level, perhaps. But if it hadn't been for you we'd have never met.'

He fell into a chair. 'And now you'll probably be lifelong friends.'

'Probably.' She set her mug down. 'You're free to join the party anytime you want, you know.'

His silence burned.

'And Travis and Joey aren't the only ones getting something out of this arrangement. I've enjoyed the company. It's been comforting to have a strapping lad like Travis stay. He's not the kind of guy Chris would mess with.'

She glanced up to find him staring at her, his eyes dark.

'*You've* had a positive impact on me too, Rico. You've made me feel safer—not just with the security system, but insisting I take self-defence classes. So thank you.'

'No problem.'

She clapped her hand. 'Now, about the café…'

He straightened, instantly alert. 'Problems?'

'Far from it! We're operating at a tidy profit. More than we'd originally projected.'

'That's good news.'

She'd known he'd be pleased. He planned to plug every penny back into the programme. 'I think it's time to start training up a new set of boys.'

'It's too soon.'

'No, it's not. If all of our current boys are offered jobs after our gala event—'

'Then we'll just start from scratch.'

'So we'll close the café for a week while I give the new boys some basic training?'

He frowned. 'Will that be necessary?'

'Yes. Our clientele have come to expect a certain level of service and I want to keep delivering on that promise. I wouldn't start the new boys all at once. I'd stagger their training. They wouldn't have too many shifts to start with, but enough for them to learn the basics.'

He nodded. 'That makes sense.'

'Also...' She gripped her hands in her lap. 'Travis wants to stay.'

'That's not the point of this programme. It's out of the question.'

'I need someone who is experienced in the kitchen, Rico.'

'Then train up one of—'

'It's not possible to fully train someone from scratch in two or three months. Besides, at the end of my year you will need someone to replace me, and Travis is the perfect candidate.'

He opened his mouth.

'Furthermore,' she added, before he could say anything, 'it'd make a great success story for the local papers. It'd be great publicity for the programme.'

He scowled at her. 'Why won't you stay for the two years?'

'Because I have things to do. Dreams to put into action.'

His scowl deepened.

'Look, Rico, they might seem trivial beside all that you're doing, but they're important to me and I won't let you belittle them.'

He blinked. 'I wasn't meaning to belittle them.'

'And, if you're serious about moving to seven-day trading, rather than hire another café manager why not trial Travis?'

His eyes suddenly narrowed. 'Are they really your dreams, Neen, or were they your grandfather's?'

Her jaw slackened.

'You love working at the café. Don't try to deny it.'

'I don't want to deny it.'

She leaped up, but once on her feet she didn't know what she was doing there. Retreating, perhaps, from all that tempting masculinity.

She strode to the cupboard. 'Cookie?'

When she turned he was right there—crowding her, blocking her way, forcing her to face him.

He tipped her chin up to meet his gaze. 'Do you really want to leave the café, Neen? Will having your own café really make you happier?'

She and her grandfather's dream café was so vivid in her mind. The cakes she'd cook, the exotic tropical décor, the clientele. It was so different—totally different—from the charity café. And yet…

She woke up every morning eager to greet the day and set off for work.

'Your grandfather shared with you his love of cooking. It nurtured you throughout a less than ideal childhood.'

'Oh, that's—'

His grip on her chin tightened and her words dried on her tongue.

'And you, in your turn, nurture others through your cooking. You're already living your grandfather's dream. Why can't you see that?'

His heat and his scent beat at her. Her heart pounded.

'Are you sure you're not using the practicalities of bringing that so-called dream café into being as a way of coping with your grief?'

His words sliced at her and she batted his hand away. 'That's probably exactly what I'm doing—but so what if I am? It helps!' She still missed her grandad, and nothing would ease that grief other than time, but working towards their dream café made her feel close to him. 'What does it matter? I'm not hurting anyone.'

'It could hurt *you*.'

She stilled. Swallowing, she met his gaze again.

'Instead of making a reasoned decision based on what will make you truly happy, you might find yourself locked into a course of action you start to regret.'

His words shone a light on her motives, hammered at them until they fell down and crumbled to dust. Her heart lodged in her throat. Eventually she managed to swallow it.

'You might have a point,' she finally whispered. She hadn't stopped to think. She'd simply rushed to put her plans into action. She'd wanted to make Grandad proud of her. But…he'd always been proud of her. She'd never had to prove herself to him.

Rico watched her carefully, his eyes searching her face.

She swallowed again and nodded. 'Yes, you're right. I can see now that's what *you've* done in your grief for Louis, your guilt over the mistakes you made.' She didn't want to live her life like that.

His nostrils flared. He took a step back. She suddenly found she could breathe easier, but an ache throbbed low down deep inside her.

'We're talking about you, not me.'

'Right.' She drew the word out. 'So you're excluded from all kinds of good advice and received wisdom, huh?'

'That's not what I meant.'

She moved in on him, the way he had on her earlier. When the kitchen table brought him up short, he planted his hands on his hips and pulled himself up to his full height. Neen refused to be intimidated.

'In your own life you're too scared to look closely

at the concept of job satisfaction or even life satis-faction because you know the answers you'll come back with. I think you're too scared to work towards whatever it is your heart desires because before you can follow it you'll have to forgive yourself for the mistakes you made when you were seventeen years old.'

White lines bracketed his mouth. His chest rose and fell. She ached to reach out and pull him into her arms, to soothe the agony she could see in his eyes.

'Rico, you were just a boy. Haven't you punished yourself enough? Don't you think you have a right to the same things you fight to give these boys? A life that is—'

He reached out and seized her shoulders. Her words clattered to a halt. His grip should have been hard, brutal, but even in his distress he tempered his strength.

'Don't you get it yet?' His voice shook. 'I don't *deserve* to be happy after what I did. These boys have legitimate excuses for going off the rails. They're from broken families. They've suffered violence and abuse and neglect. I never had any such excuse. I came from a loving family who...'

Who'd put too much pressure on him.

His grip tightened. 'I wasted my chances.'

She saw then that if he'd had less honour—a less finely tuned sense of responsibility and compassion—he'd have been able to move on from this long ago.

'I don't deserve another chance.'

Her eyes stung. 'Oh, Rico, that's not true.' She could barely push the words out for the lump in her throat.

His face softened. He released her and briefly reached out to brush her cheek with the backs of his fingers. 'Don't waste your sympathy on me.' His lips twisted into a self-derisory smile. 'You know I'll only use it against you.'

No, he wouldn't. And even if he did she wouldn't care.

That was the moment she realised that she cared more for this man than was wise.

She tossed her head, unable to look at that thought too closely when he watched her with those dark eyes. She'd consider it later, when she was alone. She'd come up with a plan to counter it. She was *not* going to jump from the proverbial frying pan into the fire.

'Haven't you learned your lesson yet, D'Angelo? You should know by now that you can't railroad me into anything.'

He gave a soft laugh. 'You telling me you're *not* going to sign an extension on your contract? You've given your heart to the place, and you're deluding yourself if you think otherwise.'

She'd given her heart to more than just the café.

She glanced into the living room at Monty and planted her hands on her hips. 'I'll tell you what I'm *not* going to do.' She lifted her chin. 'I'm not going to rush into any major decisions about my future until I'm sure my judgement isn't clouded by either grief or fear.'

His face darkened momentarily at her oblique reference to Chris, but then it cleared and he smiled at her. A genuine smile from his very depths. It robbed her of breath.

'Good for you.'

They stared at each other. Neen's body shuddered as she dragged air back into her lungs. She should move away from him, but her limbs had grown heavy and languid. The greedy way he surveyed her lips sent a roaring hunger firing through her. Rico had promised never to kiss her again, but what would he do if *she* kissed *him*?

What would he do if she reached up on tiptoe and pressed her length against him, touched her lips to his?

'Neen...' he growled.

But he didn't step away, and she swayed towards him. His hands reached out to curl around her shoulders.

There was the sound of a key in the front door... The front door opening...

Neen and Rico jumped apart. She swung away to catch her breath, to school her pulse, to lecture her wayward mind.

Travis strode into the kitchen. He stilled when he saw Rico. 'Hey, Rico.'

'Travis.'

He glanced at Neen and back at Rico. 'Did something happen tonight?'

She blinked. Good grief, Travis wasn't going to come across all paternal on her, was he?

'Has Chris tried something?'

She relaxed. 'Heck, no. Rico dropped around to give us this.' She passed him the document that held pride of place on the kitchen counter. 'In celebration, Joey and I talked him into staying for dinner.'

She watched Travis as he read the letter and wondered if his reactions would mirror her earlier ones—lack of comprehension followed by disbelief and then tentative hope.

'But this…' Travis couldn't seem to finish.

'It means everything is legal and aboveboard,' Rico said.

'Mum's not going to cause trouble?'

'She's going to get some help—go to rehab.'

Travis met Rico's gaze. 'Thank you.'

'You're welcome.'

Travis shook his head. Neen's heart went out to him as she saw the expression on his face. 'You don't know what this means to us—to me and Joey.'

'Perhaps not,' Rico agreed. 'But I think I'm starting to.'

And then he shocked Neen all the way down to the bottoms of her cotton socks by pulling Travis into a rough hug.

* * *

Rico arrived at the café first thing on the morning of Melbourne Cup Day and set up two huge television screens so everyone in the café would be able to watch the race. When he was done he demanded that he be put to work. He found himself ensconced beside Travis—chopping, slicing and whisking.

Melbourne Cup Day was always the first Tuesday in November. This week they'd agreed to open on Tuesday and be closed Wednesday. It would mean Neen's weekend would be split, but she didn't seem to mind.

Today it was a case of all hands on deck to help with the setting up of the tables and the preparation and cooking of the set menu. The lunch wasn't due to be served until one-thirty, with *hors d'oeuvres* from twelve-thirty onwards, but ticketholders started turning up well before midday.

Rico might be busy helping in the kitchen, but it didn't stop him marvelling at Neen's ease and her charm with the clientele.

'Shouldn't you be out there schmoozing?' Travis said to him, not long after the first course had been served.

Undoubtedly.

Most of the crowd consisted of local businessmen, restaurateurs and hoteliers and the like, not to mention the press. He *should* be out there canvassing for support, pointing out the staff's abilities and talking the café up. He removed his apron and bit back a grimace. Neen seemed to be doing a remarkable job on her own, but it was hardly fair to leave the entire working of the room to her.

He shrugged into his suit jacket, reluctant to swap the frenetic but ordered craziness of the kitchen for hob-nobbing and business bullying. He gritted his teeth and forced himself out into the café. He stood in the doorway to scan the crowd, but really it was Neen he searched for. And when he found her he let out a pent-up breath.

He watched her and his heart started to thump. If he'd made different decisions ten years ago he might have had a chance with a woman like her. His hands clenched against the burn, the temptation and the need. He deserved to suffer them all.

Neen turned and stilled when she saw him. Even though the man at her side kept chattering away to her, she smiled and it eased some of the ache. And then she said something to the man without looking at him and moved towards Rico, obviously intent on dragging him into the fray.

He didn't feel dragged, though, as she slipped her hand into the crook of his arm and led him across to a group of businessmen. He felt…*included*. He frowned, but there was no denying that he felt part of the festivities.

Four hours later he couldn't remember the last time he'd found a business function so exhilarating…and it wasn't wholly down to the fact that all the boys had received job offers either. Nor was it due to the unmistakable interest in when the café's next recruits would be ready to show off their talents.

His gaze slid to Neen. They'd had more job offers for Travis than they could count on one hand too, but she'd remained firm in her resolution to keep him on at the café. He hadn't interfered. It surprised him, but he trusted her judgement completely where the welfare of the boys was concerned.

Just not with your welfare.

He pushed that unwelcome thought away. He'd set his course and he had no intention of deviating from it, regardless of the incentive.

Neen glanced up at him as if she could sense his gaze. She grinned. He couldn't help it. He had to grin back. She hitched her head in the direction of the kitchen and then disappeared through its swinging door. Intrigued, he followed her.

'Everything okay?'

'Okay?' She grinned like a loon. 'It's better than okay. The luncheon has been a resounding success. A triumph!'

He glanced back the way they'd come. 'There're a lot of stragglers still.'

'I think it's worth our while to humour them. We're netting ourselves a lot of goodwill out there that might pay off in the future. The thing is they want to keep drinking, which is fine, but the terms of our liquor licence state we can only serve alcohol with food.'

And all the food was eaten.

'So I was wondering if you and Travis could put together some quick nibbles?'

As she spoke she put together an antipasto platter with the speed of light.

'Parmesan pastry sticks, spiced nuts and cheese and fruit platters?' Travis suggested.

'That'd be perfect!'

'No probs at all.' Travis tossed Rico an apron.

Rico set to work, humming under his breath. His café was proving an unmitigated success. He grinned. He couldn't wait for another few months to roll around before the next gala event.

Rico stumbled in to his apartment at nearly eight o'clock, famished.

Amazingly, given all the food available at the café today, he'd barely eaten a thing. At first he'd been too nervous, and then too busy.

He strode across to the freezer and pulled out a frozen meal. He didn't even glance down to see what variety he'd grabbed. He halted with it halfway towards the microwave.

He stopped. Very slowly he turned and walked back to the fridge, opened the door. He stared at the contents he'd bought on impulse yesterday—steaks, fresh vegetables and the ingredients for a smoky barbecue sauce.

You're allowed to enjoy yourself.

He waved a hand in front of his face to dispel Neen's voice, to try and get it out of his head. But he didn't close the fridge door. Swallowing, he shoved the readymade meal back into the freezer. Would Louis care if he fixed himself something to eat? *Really?* Would he honestly resent the fact Rico might enjoy preparing a meal?

He slammed the fridge door closed.

He paced.

Of course Louis wouldn't mind. But…

He blinked. But what?

His heart pounded. He rested his forehead against the refrigerator. 'Louis, mate, I'm sorry you're not here.' With every atom of his soul he wished his friend were here, so he could cook him up a steak. 'Every day I'm a thousand times sorry.'

After a long moment he straightened and planted himself at the kitchen table. He thought over all the conversations he'd had with Neen. If he meant to be cheerful and friendly at work then he'd have to follow at least part of her advice. If he didn't he would burn out.

In fact, he wished he *was* a robot, but he wasn't, and the options as he saw them were few.

Option one: don't change and keep treating the boys the way his mother treated him. He shook his head. That wasn't an option. It wasn't the impression he meant to give.

He stiffened and his mouth dried as he gained a possible insight into his mother's behaviour. Maybe it *wasn't* constant disappointment, anger and bitterness that rolled off her in great waves, but worry and anxiety. A weight that had no business shifting lifted from his shoulders. He scrubbed both hands back through his hair. He'd consider that later.

Focus!

Option two: try and do everything. He grimaced. That was the route to burnout. When that happened—and he knew it was a *when* rather than an *if*—he wouldn't be of any use to anyone.

Option three: start taking some time out to relax. He closed his eyes and breathed in deeply.

And then he rose and started gathering ingredients from the fridge and setting them on the bench. He collected knives and a cutting board...

Rico sliced into his steak. It was tender and rare and glazed with the sauce he'd made. He lifted it to his mouth and ate. *Delicious!* He sliced into the carrots and zucchini. He relished every single mouthful.

He had two bites left when his cell phone rang.

He contemplated leaving it to go to his message bank, but habit gripped him too hard. He pulled it out. 'Rico D'Ang—'

'You need to get to Neen's right now!'

He shot to his feet. 'Travis?'

'Her apartment is on fire.'

Rico was out through the door before he'd hung up the phone.

CHAPTER TEN

NEEN WATCHED HER unit burn. Along with the rest of the residents from the complex, she watched the firemen fight to get the blaze under control. A chasm opened up inside her and she clasped Joey all the more securely to her side.

Was Chris responsible for this? A lump lodged in her throat. Not in a million years would she have thought he'd go so far.

The flames surged higher. What a mistake she'd made. Her search for love had blinded her.

The firemen trained their hoses on the flames and eventually the fire started to sputter and die, leaving behind blackness and destruction.

She'd made a mistake, but did she really deserve this?

'Neen?'

The concern in Travis's voice reached her. It was the only reason she managed to tear her gaze from the scene in front of her.

'Are you okay?'

The poor kid looked worried and completely out

of his depth. For heaven's sake, he was only seventeen! 'I'm shell-shocked, that's all.' From somewhere she dredged up something she hoped would pass for a smile. 'The unit and everything inside it are just things. Things can be replaced.'

The photographs of her grandfather! She swallowed a sob. *Don't think about that now.*

'As long as we and our neighbours are safe, that's the important thing.'

She stared at the two boys and the hole inside her grew so big it threatened to swallow her up. She'd put Travis and Joey in danger. By bringing them into her home, she'd put them in danger. What on earth had she been thinking?

'Neen! Travis! Joey!'

They all swung around. Rico strode down the driveway, his shoulders broad and his body strong with purpose. Her knees trembled and the darkness inside her backed up a couple of steps.

He didn't hesitate. He encompassed both her and Joey in a hug, his arms strong and reassuring as he pulled her against his chest and pulled Joey into his side. Freeing one hand momentarily, he reached out and briefly clasped Travis's arm. 'Thank God you're all all right.'

For a moment she just clung to him. She breathed him in and her heart-rate settled and the hole inside her started to shrink.

Stupid girl! This is what landed you in trouble

in the first place—wanting someone to love you—
wanting someone to look after you.

She stiffened. She didn't want Rico to love her.

She glanced up, took in the line of strong, masculine jaw, the even features and thickly lashed eyes, and her mouth dried. One by one she unclenched her fingers from the material of his shirt and carefully eased away from him. His eyes, full of concern, turned and surveyed her.

Concern for his café, she tried telling herself. But she couldn't make herself believe it.

'Are you okay?'

She nodded, but for the life of her she couldn't find a smile. 'I can't tell you how glad I am you're here.' She couldn't lie about that. 'But…' She gestured to her now smouldering apartment. 'There's not much you can do.'

'I intend to speak to the firemen and find out how this fire started.'

She sighed. They all knew who'd started it. Proving it, though, would be the challenge.

The firemen eventually started packing up their hoses and equipment. The fire chief spoke to the police, who'd arrived on the scene at the same time as Rico, and Rico moved over to confer with them. Neen didn't join him. She didn't want to hear what they had to say. She stayed with Travis and Joey, leaning against her car and staring at her destroyed unit. Thankfully the other units in the blocks had only suffered minor damage, but hers…

She forced herself to look away.

'Where are we going to sleep tonight?' Joey asked.

She blinked and straightened. Where indeed? 'I... um...'

'We can go back to Mum's,' Travis mumbled.

Joey didn't say anything, but he huddled in closer to her side.

'I don't think that'll be necessary.' She met Travis's gaze so he knew she meant it. 'Your mum is getting treatment, and it's probably best to not distract her from that at the moment.'

His shoulders loosened a fraction.

She bit back a sigh. 'We can stay with my parents.'

'Are they nice?' Joey whispered.

'Sure.' But the word came out high and tight.

This would provide them with exactly the ammunition they needed. It would make her beholden to them. It would give them the opportunity to present every argument under the sun as to why she should hand over Grandad's inheritance. They would do everything they could to wear her down. And she was so tired.

She closed her eyes and swallowed back a lump.

'Okay, you lot. You're coming home with me.'

Her eyes flew open to find Rico standing in front of them, jangling his car keys.

But...?

Beside her Joey straightened. No longer huddling.

No longer scared. The shadow of a smile lit Travis's face.

'We'll sort you out some longer-term accommodation tomorrow.'

She moistened her lips. 'Are you sure?'

'Of course I'm sure. What? Did you think I was going to leave you on the street?'

They weren't his responsibility, regardless of what he thought.

'It's what friends are for, Neen.'

Friends? She smiled, then. 'Thank you.'

'C'mon—I think you could all do with something warm inside you.'

She tapped her car. 'I can follow you.'

'We can come back and collect your car tomorrow, Neen. You're dead on your feet. And you've had a nasty shock,' he added when she opened her mouth.

She closed it again, hauled in a breath and nodded. 'Okay.' She'd let him take care of them tonight, but she wouldn't get used to it. She wouldn't let it go on indefinitely. She wouldn't make the same mistake twice.

Tomorrow she'd look after herself again.

They walked out to the street and then Rico slammed to a halt. 'Where's Monty?'

Her eyes filled with the tears she'd been fighting all evening.

'He must've got out somehow,' Travis said. 'The fire must've spooked him and...'

He trailed off. Neen blinked fiercely. 'The neighbours are going to keep an eye out for him.'

'He's all on his own,' Joey blurted out.

Rico pressed Joey's shoulder. 'He's a smart dog. He'll be okay.'

Who was Rico trying to kid?

Joey stared up at her. 'Is Rico right?'

'Monty will be fine,' she said, with more conviction than she felt. 'He's a dumbass dog, but they're the ones who always land on their feet. He'll find some poor sucker to look after him.'

Joey started to laugh. 'A dumbass dog. You hear that, Travis? Monty is a *dumbass* dog!'

'Spill it. How are you really doing?'

Neen sat curled into one corner of Rico's leather couch. He sat on the floor on the other side of the coffee table. There'd been an unspoken agreement between them this evening to keep a physical distance, even if they couldn't prevent their gazes from incessantly straying to the other.

Rico had fed and watered them. He'd lent them clothes and provided them with toothbrushes and toiletries. He'd given them a roof over their heads. She couldn't begin to thank him.

Travis and Joey had not long retired to the spare bedroom. Joey to sleep and Travis ostensibly to keep him company. She had a feeling Travis was trying to be tactful and leave her and Rico alone.

One glance at Rico—casual in tracksuit pants

that somehow managed to heighten the length and strength of his legs, and a T-shirt that had her constantly reassessing the depth of his chest—and she had a feeling 'alone time' with him was the last thing either she or her pulse needed.

She glanced down at her hands. 'I want to thank you for everything you've done tonight—for taking us in like you have. You've gone above and beyond.'

'You don't need to keep thanking me,' he said quietly. 'I did this because I wanted to. I was *happy* to.'

Behind the dark glitter of his eyes she recognised something more than duty and a sense of responsibility. Maybe it was friendship and a need to connect. Or maybe it was desire. All she knew was she'd never seen Rico more at ease. It made him all the more potent and enticing. And she ached to go to him, to lose herself in him. To find respite and rest in his arms. And pleasure.

She shivered and tried to bury that thought.

'What I want to know, Neen, is if you're okay.'

She closed her eyes and counted to three. She opened them again. 'I'm worried about a couple of things.'

He leaned forward, completely alert. 'Yes?'

'I never thought Chris would go this far.'

'Neen—'

'I know I'm jumping to conclusions, but it's a fairly logical conclusion to jump to—right?'

He hesitated and then nodded.

'I've unknowingly put Travis and Joey at risk

by taking them into my home. What if they'd been there when the fire started? What if they'd been hurt or—?'

He was at her side in one swift movement, his hands at her shoulders, halting her flow of words. 'Chris doesn't want to hurt you. He wants to scare you so you'll go back to him. He's had multiple opportunities to burn the unit while you were inside it—with or without Travis and Joey there.'

'But the threats are escalating. It's getting worse. I can't guarantee the boys' safety any longer. I—'

She broke off to drag a hand through her hair. He tried to pull her against his chest to comfort her, but she resisted. She disengaged herself from his grip and moved to an armchair.

He stared at her, his eyes unreadable. 'Do you think I'm going to take advantage of you?'

Her heart clenched at the flash of pain that underlaid his words. She had to swallow before she could speak. 'I can't… It's not you I don't trust, Rico. This…' She waved her hand about the room. 'Being taken care of. It's what I did with Chris.'

His chin jerked up. 'I'm not like Chris! Is that what you think?'

'No! God, no! It's me. I wanted him to love me for *me*.' She gripped her hands together. 'I wanted someone to look after me because…' Her throat threatened to close over. 'And look what a mess I got myself into. I need to look after myself, not rely on someone else to do that. I won't make the same mistake again.'

'You just want what everyone wants.'

The warmth in his voice caressed her. She had to harden her heart against it. '*You* don't.'

The silence filled with a tension that made her teeth ache. She forced her mind back on track. 'Travis and Joey—I can't risk them getting hurt. I…'

'I'll look after them.'

Her head came up.

'Travis turns eighteen next week. He and Joey can stay here till then. After that they can go into the public housing I've organised.'

'You mean tha—?' She bit the words back. 'Thank you.' She wanted to hug him.

'You're welcome to stay here too.'

'Thank you, but no.' The fewer people whose lives she risked the better. Tomorrow she'd find somewhere else to stay.

'Why did I know you were going to say that?'

He didn't, however, frown or glower at her as he would have done two or so months ago. He didn't try to argue with her or change her mind. He gave her the courtesy of respecting her decision. For some reason that made her feel better than her self-defence classes ever had.

She wanted to tell him how grateful she was for that, but every time she looked at him the words jammed in her throat and all she could think of was how solid and warm he'd been when he'd pulled her against him earlier.

And how much she wanted to hurl herself into his arms now, drag his mouth down to hers and forget about everything but touch and sensation.

'Neen—'

Her name scraped out of his throat, raw with control, and she snapped away, realising she'd been staring at him with so much naked hunger he couldn't possibly mistake what she wanted.

Raising shaking fingers to her temples, she pressed them there and tried to bring her mind back to the things they needed to discuss.

She pulled in a breath. 'Would you like me to resign?'

'Why on earth would I want that?'

One glance told her his glower was back in force.

'No way, Neen! We have an agreement.' He stabbed a finger at her. 'You signed a contract.'

'Fat lot of good that'll do either one of us if the café becomes the next target.'

'I will not let you quit.'

A tiny thread of relief trickled through her. She didn't want to leave the café. She loved working there.

She shifted on her seat. She didn't want to leave the café *yet*.

'There's a vacant "safe house" apartment in North Hobart that you can use for the time being.'

Her shoulders drooped. 'But that's on the other side of the harbour from Bellerive.'

'Why's Bellerive so important when—?' He broke off, his face gentling. 'Monty?'

She nodded.

'The neighbours will keep an eye out for him, and we can check with them every day. I'll contact the local pound…and we can scout around tomorrow to see if we can find him.'

The big doofus of a dog was out there alone. She bit her lip. He'd never spent a night outside before, let alone one on his own.

'He'll turn up, Neen.'

As long as he wasn't flattened on the side of the road somewhere.

'There's nothing more we can do tonight.'

That much was true.

'You must be beat. Why don't you head off to bed?'

He'd given her his bedroom. He was sleeping on the couch. She knew further argument on that subject was pointless. 'Rico, I want to say again how much I—'

'If you thank me one more time I'll kiss you.'

She stiffened.

He watched her.

She moistened her lips. All she had to do was say thank you again and he'd…

Her heart pounded against her ribs and her skin

prickled with a sudden rush of heat. *Fire. Emotional. Don't be stupid.*

Very slowly she rose and backed away. 'Uh… goodnight, Rico.'

'Night, Neen.'

She closed her eyes against the disappointment that threaded his voice and bolted for his bedroom.

'Bloody hell!' Rico turned his back on the television monitor to drag a hand down his face.

'You know who they are?'

Rafe, the owner of the security firm Rico had hired to kit out Neen's place, stared at him, his expression grim. Having a security camera fitted to Neen's carport had been a last-minute decision. Rico hadn't actually expected it to bear fruit.

He glanced at the screen one last time and nodded.

'I won't be able to keep this from the police, Rico.'

'No.'

'From the look on your face, though, this isn't a welcome discovery.'

'Neen's going to be gutted.' He didn't doubt that for a single moment. 'Can you give me two hours before you take that to the police?'

'Can do.'

'Thanks, Rafe. I owe you.'

'Just doing my job.'

Rico started for the door.

'Hey, Rico, you wouldn't be interested in joining

a baseball team by any chance, would you? Me and the lads are putting a team together for the summer comp.'

Rico turned and blinked. 'Me?'

Rafe shrugged. 'You look fit.'

He started to refuse, to say he wouldn't have the time, but Neen's voice sounded in his head; he saw her finger wagging at him. 'I...uh...' He shifted the weight from one leg to the other. 'I haven't played since school.'

'Join the club.' Rafe shrugged. 'I know you work in a field where the odd emergency comes up at a moment's notice. We can work around that.'

Rico suddenly saw the offer for what it was—a gesture of friendship.

His stomach started to churn. How many like offers had he not recognised in the past? He forced his chin up. 'In that case I'm definitely interested. Shoot me through the details.'

Rafe grinned. 'Talk soon, buddy.'

As he left Rafe's office, Rico found himself grinning too.

Until he remembered what he'd just seen on the security video.

Rico's heart burned as if a thousand needles spiked through it as Neen watched his copy of the security tape. Tears filled her eyes and spilled over, but she wiped them away without a sound. When the tape finished she eased back in her seat and breathed in deeply. Her pallor made the needles spike through him harder and fiercer.

Eventually she glanced round at him. 'You recognised them from the photo on the hall table?'

'Yes.'

She swallowed. 'They must really want Grandad's money, huh?'

He sat beside her and squeezed her hand. 'Neen, I'm really sorry.'

She nodded, but she didn't say anything. He wanted to pull her into his arms and make everything right for her. The way she'd pulled out of his arms last night stopped him.

Neen didn't want any complications.

He frowned. Neither did he.

'I'm shocked!' The words were blurted out, as if she couldn't hold them back…and as if she loathed their obviousness. 'I mean, not in ten million years would I have ever thought… I mean, how on earth could they do that to anyone…let alone their only child?'

Her pain cut at him.

'But…'

'But?'

She was silent for several long moments. She pulled both hands back through her hair. Eventually she met his gaze again. 'If Chris didn't start the fire, then maybe he didn't throw the paint on my house or slash my tyres or…or any of those other things.'

Exactly what Rico had been thinking.

'Maybe he's not stalking me at all.' She frowned. 'And if that's the case then it means…' She glanced up at him. 'It means my search for love, my desire to be important to someone, *didn't* cause all of this.'

'None of this has been your fault!'

She shook her head. 'It took me a long while to recognise Chris's possessiveness for what it was. When I did, I ended our relationship.' Her frown started to clear. 'That was a sensible decision. *Smart.*'

She'd get no argument from him on that. 'Exactly.'

The dazed light in her eyes was slowly replaced by a new clarity. 'I've been blaming myself for not having come to that decision sooner, but I'm not a fool or an idiot. I've just been finding my way and trying to live my life the best way I can, like every other person on the planet. I might've made a poor judgement call where Chris was concerned, but it wasn't *that* bad.'

She leaped up and started to pace. Rico rose too.

She swung to him. 'Which is exactly what you've been trying to tell me.'

He shrugged. He had no intention of saying *I told you so*.

'I was never in danger. My parents have been playing on my insecurities until I've blown them out of all proportion.' She stopped dead. 'I can't tell you how freeing it is to realise that.'

And then she walked over to him, flung her arms round him and hugged him fiercely. He wrapped his arms around her, every cell in his body coming alive at the contact. He never wanted to let her go. It took all his strength to keep his hands where they should be.

Her breath quickened. So did his.

She softened against him. He started to harden.

With a yelp she jumped back, her cheeks pink and pretty. 'Sorry, I—'

'Nothing to apologise for,' he ground out.

She looked everywhere but at him. He told himself it was a blessing as he fought to get his body back under control. He glanced at his watch and bit back a curse. He needed to get this conversation back on track. 'Neen, about your parents…'

She turned back.

He wished he could spare her this. 'We're not going to be able to prevent them from being charged.' He wasn't sure how she'd feel about that. 'At the very least they'll be charged with criminal damage.'

Her eyes swirled with a mixture of emotions. 'I won't be pressing charges myself, though.'

He hadn't thought she would. 'We have roughly an hour before the police are given a copy of the tape you just watched.'

The tiniest smile touched her lips. 'You thought I might want to see them first?'

Did she?

Her hands gripped the tops of her arms until her fingers turned white. 'This might sound pathetic, but I don't want to go there on my own.'

'That was never an option.'

'Oh, they won't threaten me *physically*.'

He wasn't taking that chance.

Suddenly she smiled, as if she'd read something she liked in his face. It lightened something inside him.

He took her arm. 'C'mon, I'll drive. You can give me directions.'

They arrived at Neen's parents' house on the outskirts of Hobart thirty minutes later. Rico glanced around at the rows of dog kennels, runs and exercise yards, and winced at the cacophony of barking.

Neen had started to lead the way towards the house, but suddenly stopped dead, tilted her head to one side and then redirected her steps towards the kennels.

'Monty!' She raced forward to unlock his cage and half caught him as he tried to leap into her arms.

How on earth she'd recognised his bark through the racket Rico had no idea. She dropped to her knees and let him lick her face and bounce all around her without once remonstrating with him.

'Neen!'

Neen rose. 'Heel,' she murmured to Monty, who immediately sat as close to Neen's left leg as he could get. 'Mum. Dad,' she said, as a middle-aged couple reached them.

She made no move to kiss their cheeks or hug

them, which he understood. But they made no move to kiss *her*, which he didn't get at all.

They glanced at him. 'This is my boss and friend Rico D'Angelo. My parents,' she said shortly. 'Jack and Elaine Cuthbert.'

They nodded at each other. Rico had to hold himself in check and remain where he was, when all he wanted to do was seize both of them and shake them till their teeth rattled.

She gestured to Monty. 'I should've known you wouldn't leave him to burn.'

Her mother drew herself up. 'What nonsense are you talking, Neen? He was brought in this morning and—'

'Stop lying. *Please* stop lying.'

Neen didn't shout, which somehow only made it worse. Rico moved in a fraction closer to give her whatever moral support he could.

'I know you're responsible for last night's fire. There was a security camera. You were caught on tape.'

The older couple both paled.

Neen tucked her hair behind her ears. 'I take it the plan was to scare me into returning home? To create a sense of obligation in me so I'd hand Grandad's money over to you without a whimper?'

The way she twisted her hands twisted Rico's heart.

Her mother leaned forward, her face contorting. 'That money should've come to *me*!'

'I offered to give you half,' Neen cried. 'Why couldn't you be content with that?'

'Half?' her mother spat. 'We deserve the *full* amount! We're doing good work here! This place needs the money more than you do, and—'

'That's utter rot!' Neen's whole body shook.

Monty whined. Without looking at him she made a hand gesture and he promptly lay down, but his head remained lifted and alert.

'Rot?' Her father surged forward. 'What are you talking about?'

Rico shifted his shoulder a fraction to shield Neen. If either one of them tried to so much as pluck a single hair from her head…

'Running this dog shelter is the only thing the two of you have ever wanted to do. It has nothing to do with being compassionate to four-legged creatures or being self-sacrificing for the greater good. You just package it that way to get more money out of people…and more kudos—*Oh, those Cuthberts. Aren't they good people?* But you're both as greedy and grasping as any capitalist corporate tycoon. Well, I'm not playing your game anymore. My heart's desire is just as important as yours. And so is Grandad's! And, believe me, after the stunts you've been pulling, no judge is going to grant you a *cent* of his money.'

The older couple both took a step back. 'You're going to have us charged?'

Neen's shoulders sagged for a moment. Finally she

shook her head. 'It seems I at least still have some
family feeling. I won't be pressing charges. I can't
say, however, that the police and the owner of the
unit you burned will be quite so lenient.'

Her mother's jaw dropped. 'But...'

Neen moved closer to Rico. Some sixth sense
warned him she was nearing the end of her strength.
He lifted his chin and widened his stance, did everything he could to look mean and intimidating.

'It's out of Neen's hands.' A police car had pulled
up into the driveway beside his. 'I advise you to get
good legal representation.' He handed Neen's father
the business card for a local attorney.

Her father glanced from the card to the police
car and then wildly at the kennels. 'But the dogs!'

'I'll call the RSPCA,' Neen said. 'They'll take
care of it.'

He and Neen watched as her parents were led
away. When she glanced up at him, the pain in her
eyes made him suck in a breath.

'They didn't even apologise,' she whispered.

'They're obsessed.' He gestured to the kennels.
'And it's skewed their thinking.'

'Do you think they ever really loved me?'

She'd tried to make her voice casual but it broke
on the last word. With a cut-off oath, Rico pulled
her against his chest.

CHAPTER ELEVEN

IT TOOK ALL of Neen's strength not to cry, but it left her with no strength to resist Rico and the comfort he offered. She melted against him. The warmth and solidity of his chest and the way he wrapped his arms around her kept her anchored. He provided her with a momentary haven from the confusion and disarray that surrounded her.

She closed her eyes and breathed him in until the hard fist around her heart loosened and the ache in her throat eased.

She wished she could stay like this all day, harboured in his arms. She stayed longer than she should, but the rhythmic stroke of his hand on her hair told her he had all the time in the world. And she chose to believe it.

Eventually, regretfully, she eased herself away. She glanced up at him and tried to smile.

'Neen, they're idiots. Absolute idiots.'

'Dear Rico.' She reached up and cupped his face. He stared back at her with those intense dark eyes and chiselled cheekbones, and she finally grasped that she'd fallen utterly and hopelessly in love with this man.

Well, why wouldn't she? He had such a big heart. He tried to do so much good. He'd started making connections with people like Travis and Joey. And with her. He'd helped her find a sense of direction. He'd helped her take back control of her life. Of *course* she'd fallen in love with him!

And she had no idea what to do about it. Did she tell him? Did she try and make him fall in love with her too? Should she fight for him or let him walk away?

Her hand remained at his cheek and his vitality and power flooded into her. A pulse kicked to life deep inside her. His eyes darkened further and his breath quickened. The pulse at the base of his jaw pounded. She stared at it for a moment, and then back into his eyes.

Holding her gaze, he pressed a kiss to her palm and a tremor ran through her. She loved him. The words ran through her over and over. She loved him and she wanted him.

Slowly, almost questioningly, as if to give her plenty of time to back away, his lips descended towards hers. Neen hovered between heartbeats, wanting him so much she was afraid to move in case he changed his mind. And then she lifted her face in silent invitation and he closed the distance between them.

Her lips parted at the first contact. She needed the

feel and the taste of him too much to pretend otherwise. He held her lightly, no rush or urgency in his touch. His lips moved over hers as if he had all day to memorise their shape and their texture.

Neen knew no such patience. She slid one arm around his neck while her other fisted in his shirt to pull him closer, urging him to deepen the kiss. A rumble of approval broke from his chest, but he pulled back to kiss a path to her ear.

'We have all the time in the world, Neen.' He pressed kisses to the corner of her mouth, her eyelids, her temples.

'And we have this moment right now.' She seized his face in her hands and pulled his lips down to hers, her tongue making a bold exploration of the inner line of his lower lip.

Rico's well-mannered facade crumbled. He dragged her against him with a groan, almost pulling her off her feet, his tongue tangling with hers. She wanted to laugh and cry. She wanted to fling her arms wide and let the wind rush against her.

And she wanted to savour every single moment of kissing him.

She had no idea how long they lost themselves in each other, but when Rico finally lifted his head her lips throbbed and pulsed. She ran her tongue across them and tasted Rico there. Divine and devastating.

He rested his forehead against hers and dragged in several breaths. She did too.

'Neen...'

He eased back to smile down at her. His smile was full of care and concern and she fell in love with him all over again, because it also held a hint of happiness. And that gave her hope.

'Neen, you've had a big shock today.'

She drew in a breath. 'And you don't want to take advantage of me?'

'That just about sums it up.'

'I want to take full and frank advantage of *you*.'

He grinned, and her heart soared and ached and hammered.

'But…' She wasn't ready to tell him how she felt. She needed to examine this state of affairs when her mind had cleared. But he deserved a modicum of honesty from her. She let her hands drift down his chest, relishing the feel of him beneath her fingertips. 'But if we were to make love the encounter would mean something to me.'

He sobered. 'It would mean something to me too.'

How much would it mean to him, though? She suspected he couldn't answer that yet.

She nodded. 'It may, in fact, mean more to me.'

'And you don't want to risk that?'

She was absolutely willing to risk it—but not if it blew her chance with him. Instinct told her she'd only get the one chance. 'I'm just not sure you're ready for that. If we make love I will be emotionally invested.' Who was she kidding? She was *already* emotionally invested. 'I'd want you to be emotionally invested too.'

She saw the exact moment his memories of Louis hit him. Her heart sank to her feet and flapped about like a dying fish. Gently she disengaged herself from his arms. 'I think you need to contemplate that first.'

Drag me into your arms and tell me I'm all you want!

He nodded. 'You're right.'

Her heart didn't even have the energy left to flap. She wouldn't give up. She'd give him time to mull over her words. She'd fight another day. But not today.

She gritted her teeth and resisted the urge to throw herself into his arms and settle for whatever scraps he offered her. She needed to be away from him. *Fast.* She needed her fingers to be busy with other work.

'I best ring the RSPCA and a few of the other animal protection agencies to come and take care of the dogs. We better count how many there are here and make sure they all have plenty of water while we're at it.'

Rico nodded again. 'I'll get on that right away.'

As he walked away, she told herself she hadn't lost the war. There were lots of battles in a war. She had every intention of making it as hard as she could for Rico to walk away from her—to walk away from *them*.

'Is it all sorted, then?'

For the past two weeks Rico had been skirting

around her—*them*—practically ignoring her, so she nearly dropped her handbag in surprise when she saw him sitting on a stool in the kitchen.

'Almost.' She continued through to her locker to stow her things.

'Neen, were there any problems?'

'Not a single one.' She finally turned to meet his gaze, wondering if her heart was in her eyes and if he could read it. If he could tell how much she wanted him.

How much she loved him.

Her hands clenched. Why couldn't he get over his guilt about Louis and embrace life again? Why couldn't he show himself the same understanding and magnanimity that he did to the boys?

He stared back at her, his eyes hooded. She knew he was here because he cared, because he wanted to make sure everything had gone smoothly at the solicitor's for her today. But she wanted—*needed*—more. And she didn't know how much longer she was prepared to wait.

'Everything went exactly as I hoped it would.'

'I'm glad.'

She swung to Travis. 'Thanks for covering for me. I know you have an appointment up at Joey's school this afternoon. Why don't you take off early and go get ready for it?'

He threw her a grateful smile. 'It hasn't been too busy, so I'll take you up on that. Thanks, Neen. I'll catch you both later.'

'He's gone from strength to strength since he was given custody of Joey.'

Rico had fast-tracked that.

'I don't want to talk about Travis, Neen. I want to talk about *you*.'

Her heart surged into her throat. She swallowed. 'Let me just make sure everything's shipshape out in the café first.'

A quick glance around the café told her that her two most recent recruits were handling the small crowd perfectly.

'Let me know if you need a hand,' she ordered with a pat to both their shoulders, before returning to the kitchen. And Rico.

'Now, precisely what did you want to discuss?' She didn't kid herself it would be anything other than business.

'Your grandfather's inheritance is finally yours?'

'Yes. All the documents were signed and the money is being transferred to my bank account.' Her parents' attorney had advised them to cease all claim to her inheritance immediately. He was hoping their previously exemplary records, combined with an appropriate show of remorse, would work in their favour.

'And Chris?'

'I've had the restraining order removed. He was responsible for raising all my suspicions in the first place with his initial refusal to leave me alone, but he never threw the paint or slashed my tyres. It's been something of a wake-up call for him, though. He's getting counselling to get his control issues under…uh…control.'

Rico scowled, but he didn't say anything.

'So as you can see, Rico—' she lifted her hands '—everything is finally coming together in my world.'

He stared at her, his gaze devouring her in a way that made her chest tighten and her pulse flutter.

He snapped upright from his stool and swung away from her. 'So at the end of your contract you'll leave to set up your own café?'

Something inside her snapped at that. She leaned forward and poked him in the shoulder. 'What do you *want* from me?'

He turned. His mouth opened and closed but no sound came out.

'You're not a stupid man.' She glared at him. 'You must know how I feel about you.'

Rico stared at Neen—at the wild recklessness in her eyes—and wished he'd just stayed away.

Only…

He hadn't been able to.

'I *love* you, Rico.'

The despair in her face, the pain that stretched through her voice, beat at him, and he had to close his eyes.

'And, if the way you've been avoiding me since

that day at my parents' place is anything to go by, it's obvious you're running away from that.'

His eyes rocked open. The memory of that soul-scorching kiss rose through him for the hundredth—the thousandth—time. He wanted this woman. He craved her in every molecule of his being. But he couldn't have her.

'And yet, even knowing how I feel about you, you want me to remain at the café, where I'll be forced to see you on a regular basis? You think that's *kind*?'

It was exactly what he wanted. But he saw the selfishness of it too. But to let Neen go…?

His mouth filled with ashes. 'I…I… Neen, I'm sorry.'

She moistened her tongue and need pounded through him. 'Why?' she whispered. 'Why won't you give us a chance?'

'Louis,' he croaked. 'I have no right to enjoy what he never can.' Family, children, love—they were all lost to him. All he could do was atone and hope that somehow it counted.

'Louis is dead, Rico. You're not.'

He flinched away from her.

'You have a duty to live your life to the fullest. You owe Louis that much for being the one to survive! For pity's sake, you didn't *force* him to take the heroin. He did it of his own free will.'

'That's a crazy way of thinking!'

'Burying yourself and punishing yourself—that's what's crazy! It won't bring Louis back. It doesn't change a darn thing. And can you honestly tell me Louis would want you to turn your back on life? Is that what you'd have wanted for him if your positions had been reversed? For Louis to immolate himself on an altar of guilt?'

Of course it wasn't. But…

His mind went blank, scrabbling to find a valid argument but coming up with nothing. His hand clenched. He had no right to the things Neen was offering.

But it didn't stop him wanting those things with every fibre of his being.

'And *I* don't deserve to be punished because *you* can't come to terms with your past!'

Her words slashed at him. He dragged a hand down his face and tried to breathe through the constriction in his lungs. Neen didn't deserve any kind of punishment, and certainly none of his making.

She'd get over him. Surely she'd…

He glanced at her and his gut churned harder. She *loved* him. And he was hurting her, breaking her heart. The steel inside him wavered. He craved to make her happy, to give her everything she wanted. His heart pounded. His mouth dried. A pulse hammered through him.

'Neen, what vision do you have for us?' The words left him on a ragged breath.

Her face softened. 'All we need to do is love each other and the rest will fall into place.'

Love each other? Oh, he loved her, all right. There'd never been any doubt about that.

'Can't you just trust that much, Rico?'

He fell back to the stool, planted his elbows on the bench and rested his head in his hands. Him and Neen? Could they make it work? Could he make it work for her while still focusing on everything he needed to achieve and staying true to Louis's memory?

He pushed past the nausea pounding through him. Him and Neen? Could they…?

He had a sudden vision of working with her, not exactly side by side…

He lifted his head, but he no longer saw the kitchen in front of him. His heart surged against his ribs. Him and Neen… He could continue working with at-risk youth. Neen could carry on managing the café and making it a sparkling success. So successful that between them they could open another one, and another one after that! With Neen at his side he could accomplish so much more.

He swung to her, reached for her and pulled her into the vee of his legs, his arms circling her waist. 'I've been such an idiot! I love you! You *know* I love you, right?'

Her eyes widened, her breath hitched and her eyes filled. She didn't say anything, just nodded.

His hands tightened at her waist. 'You're right. We *can* have it all.'

She threw her head back then and laughed. The

sound lifted his heart even as the clean line of her mouth beckoned. 'Of *course* we can!'

'We will make an unstoppable team.'

Two lines appeared on her forehead. 'What do you mean?'

'We can accomplish so much together! We can achieve big things!' The boys they'd save... The hope they'd give...

His mind raced with plans and it took him a moment to recognise the dawning horror in her face.

'What are you talking about?' she asked.

He took her face in his hands. 'We can create a whole chain of charity cafés. We can offer badly needed jobs and opportunities. You were right!' He pressed a kiss to her lips. 'All I needed to do was trust my love for you and the rest would follow.'

He tried to pull her closer, aching to kiss her with all the intensity raging inside him, but she broke out of his grasp and backed up, staring at him as if she'd never seen him before.

He rose, his heart hammering. 'What?'

He'd fight whatever had spooked her.

'I thought you understood what I was asking of you, Rico, but you obviously don't. I won't come second to your job. I've been through all that with my parents and I'm not doing it again.'

'What are you talking about? I *love* you.'

'No, you don't. If you did, you'd put me first.'

He went cold all over. She wanted him to give up

his job? 'What about you putting *my* needs first?' he shot back, stung.

'I am.' Her eyes filled with tears. 'I will not be party to you flaying yourself alive every single day. I will not be your consolation for that.'

Fear and darkness rose through him in equal measure. She'd given him a vision—a glorious, seductive vision of a future he wanted with all his might—and now she was taking it away.

'*Love*, Rico? I think not. I don't think you even know the meaning of the word anymore.'

She started to turn away, and then she swung back. She pressed her hand to his chest. Beneath it his heart pounded, trying to reach her, trying to find a way to make her stay with him.

'What do you want in *here*, Rico? That's what I want to be part of—not this half-life you're living now.'

And then she turned and left, leaving him more alone than he'd ever been.

Rico spent the next five days moving in a fog. It was as if a thick morass of apathy and dejection surrounded him, protecting him from the anguish of Neen's rejection.

Each day, though, a little of the fog lifted, leaving a hard, burning anger in its wake. Anger at Neen. Anger at himself and Louis for their utter stupidity as seventeen-year-olds. Anger at himself now, in the present.

He spent the spare moments of the week following pounding the pavement, lifting weights and completing endless sets of push-ups and sit-ups.

It didn't help.

He stayed away from Neen and the café. That didn't help either. One day he even stood on the corner opposite the café so he could watch Neen close up for the night. That definitely didn't help. It disgusted him too—filled him with shame when he recalled the way Chris had hounded her.

On the third Saturday after her declaration of love and subsequent rejection of him, Rico stalked out of his apartment, bought a recipe book and a whole load of ingredients and spent the afternoon cooking up a storm.

That helped a bit. Just as Neen had said it would.

'For Pete's sake,' he growled aloud. 'She doesn't have all the answers.' He fell into his sofa and glared around the room.

He wasn't sure why he spoke out loud, only that the silence in his apartment seemed oppressive. He hadn't noticed that silence until Travis and Joey had left.

He missed them too. He leaped up to pace the length of the room, rolling his shoulders and trying to rid himself of an indeterminate itch. Before he'd met Neen his life had been neat and tidy—orderly. Everything in its place and—

The oven timer buzzed and with a curse he didn't

try to smother he wheeled into the kitchen to pull
out the two trays of savoury pastries he'd assembled.

He set them on the bench and stared at them in a
combination of awe and astonishment.

They weren't particularly symmetrical, at least
not like the picture in the recipe book, but they smelt
divine and *he'd* made them. *Him.* His mouth started
to water.

Neen mightn't have all the answers, but she was
right about this. Cooking fortified something inside
him. It recharged and restored him.

Okay, so she was right about the way he'd been
holding himself aloof from people too. The friendship he'd struck up with Travis now bolstered him,
as did the avuncular relationship he'd developed with
Joey. Cutting himself off had been bad for his job.
He could see what she'd been trying to tell him. He'd
become single-minded and driven, like her parents,
and—

He flinched at that thought. Their obsession had
hurt Neen so badly, but his desire to keep at-risk
youth off the streets didn't hurt anyone.

His mouth went dry. *It didn't!*

He recalled Rafe's overture of friendship and
thought again of the similar multiple overtures made
towards him in the last few years. Overtures he'd
ruthlessly ignored in order to focus on the things
he'd deemed important.

And then he saw boys, multiple boys like Joey,
who'd just needed a hug. And he hadn't hugged them.

His hand clenched. Results—that was what he'd focused on. Results rather than people. He'd wanted to get the boys off the streets and safe. He hadn't understood that there were more important things, like human connection and friendship.

For a moment he could feel Neen's hand pressed against his heart. *What do you want in here, Rico?*

He took one of the trays of pastries to the table, sat and ate the lot. One by one, popping them into his mouth, chewing, savouring, swallowing and finding a new strength with each mouthful. By the time he'd finished them he knew exactly what he wanted.

He glanced at his watch. Six p.m. on a Saturday evening. He knew exactly where to find his heart's desire.

Monty completely ignored the ball she threw to him. He raced instead straight past her. What the—?

Oh, good grief. Who was he going to molest now?

She spun, with a screeching *Sit!* on her tongue that never made it fully out of her mouth.

Rico.

Her pulse skittered and dipped. Her chest grew so tight all she wanted to do was sink to the sand and curl up into a tiny ball. Seeing him tore at something deep inside her, and each searing rip stole more of her vitality.

Oh, right—and not seeing him has been a whole barrel of laughs, has it?

He made Monty sit before petting him, just as

she'd shown him. When the goof of a dog rolled onto his back, Rico scratched his stomach.

She glanced away from those lean brown fingers and all their promise.

'Hello, Neen.'

His voice came from right beside her. She lifted her chin and met his gaze. 'Hello, Rico.'

Monty loped into the water and barked at the waves. The silence on the beach between her and Rico grew. It stretched and tightened and made her ache.

'You wanted to see me?' she finally managed.

He shook his head, dragged a hand back through his hair. 'I haven't rehearsed anything.'

She blinked.

'And now I don't know how to start this darn conversation without just lurching into it.'

His skin was tinged an odd grey, but the rest of him glowed with vigour, as if he'd spent a lot of time outdoors recently. Concern for him warred with self-preservation.

She folded her arms. 'Then just lurch into it.'

He gave a decisive nod and planted his feet. 'You asked me what it was I really wanted…in here.' He touched a hand to his chest. 'And, Neen, now I know.'

Her heart hammered. The beach tilted. She moved up to the dry sand and sat.

He followed. 'Are you okay?'

This man could bare her to her very soul. He

could crush her with one word. What he was about to tell her would clinch her future.

'Please don't get my hopes up, Rico. I…I just don't think I could stand it.'

He fell to his knees in front of her. He cupped her face. 'Sweetheart, I have no intention of hurting you.'

His endearment burned through her. She wished she could believe him, but…

She removed his hands from her face. 'Not on purpose, perhaps.'

He subsided to the sand beside her. 'I'll tell you what I want—what I really want in my heart—and then you can decide if that makes me the kind of man you could build a life with.'

Words were impossible. All she could do was nod.

'Neen, I want to cook.'

Well, that was a no-brainer. But would he have the courage to follow that desire?

'I cooked these little pastries today and it was brilliant. *They* were brilliant.'

He had? She sat up straighter.

He turned to face her more fully. 'I want to cook and I want to have friends. I want to laugh. I want to make my life better, bigger, richer.' He hauled in a breath. 'I want to go to parties and enjoy them rather than scoping out the crowd to see who I can hit up for sponsorship or donations.'

She stared at him. Was this Rico—workaholic

extraordinaire—talking? 'Go on,' she urged when he stopped.

'I want a family.' His hands clenched. 'I want children who will keep me on my toes, who I can pass on good strong ethics to—but also a love of life. I want a wife who'll make sure I don't take myself too seriously. A woman who'll make my life bigger, better, richer. A woman who'll love me with all she has, Neen. The way you love me.'

Her heart pounded up into her throat.

'When I find her I will cherish her forever. I will do my best to become the man she needs, the man she wants me to be. I love you, Neen, and I want that life with *you*.'

She gripped her hands together. 'Do you know the man I want you to be?'

'You want me to be happy.'

He said it so simply it took her breath away. Finally she allowed herself to hope.

Spinning around so she knelt in the sand beside him, she said, 'What about Louis?'

He held her gaze. 'I will always regret what happened. I wish it hadn't. I wish I'd made different choices back then.' He paused. 'But even if I had, it doesn't mean Louis would've. I'd never considered that before, and in a way it's freed me. It's made me realise the only thing I can control is my own actions.' He pulled in a breath, his gaze never wavering from hers. 'It's time to stop living in the past. I'm not saying I won't have bad days, when I struggle with that, but I...I mean to try.'

She swore even her eyeballs pulsed.

'I've realised that if I wanted to make you happy I had to be whole. I haven't felt whole since Louis died, Neen. I've been too afraid to try in case I let someone else down. But for you I'll risk anything.'

'What about your job—the way you seem to use it to punish yourself? What about that?'

For a moment his lips almost twitched into a smile. 'You made me see what a machine I'd become. All I was focused on was getting kids off the street and safe. I wanted to do something positive, make a good difference. But watching you with Travis and Joey—heck, with all the boys—made me see you had a greater impact on them than I'd ever had.'

She drew back. 'That's nonsense! You made the café a reality. Without you...' She shook her head. It didn't bear thinking about.

He leaned towards her. 'I want to be on the inside now. Not on the outside.'

She couldn't help herself then. She launched herself into his arms. They fell back on the sand in a tangle of limbs, with Neen sprawled on top of him. She kissed him. 'Welcome home, Rico.'

He grinned up at her, his hand trailing a tantalising path down her spine. 'I'm going to ask you to marry me soon.'

'And I'm going to say yes.'

He sobered. His hands stilled. 'Don't you want to know what I plan to do workwise?'

She shook her head. 'It doesn't matter what you choose to do now, because you'll be doing it for the right reasons.'

Without warning he rolled her over. 'I want to tell you anyway.'

He pressed against her in the most delightful way imaginable. She wriggled against him, revelling in the way his eyes darkened. 'I didn't mean to imply I wasn't interested.'

He grinned. 'I want to open my own café. I'm going to learn to cook, and I'm going to employ some of our boys. Wanna join me?'

She started to laugh. 'Actually, Rico, if it's all the same to you I want to stay at the charity café. I love working there.'

His eyes widened, and then he threw his head back with a laugh. 'I *knew* it. You're hooked! That place is perfect for you.' He ran a finger down her cheek. 'Sweetheart, I just want you to do whatever will make you happy.'

She wrapped her arms around his neck. 'Rico, *you're* what makes me happy.'

They fell into each other then. Only surfacing when a wet dog and spraying sand interrupted them.

'You were right, Neen. I'm definitely a man who's in need of a dog.' He helped her to her feet and then clicked Monty's lead to his collar. 'C'mon, let's go home.'

Home. She nestled in close to his side, relishing the word. 'I was thinking salmon and asparagus crêpes would be just the thing for dinner tonight.'

'Do I get to be in charge of the whisk?'

She grinned up at him. 'I'm counting on it.'

* * * * *

REQUEST YOUR
FREE BOOKS!

2 FREE NOVELS
FROM THE ROMANCE COLLECTION
PLUS 2 FREE GIFTS!

YES! Please send me 2 FREE novels from the Romance Collection and my 2 FREE gifts (gifts are worth about $10). After receiving them, if I don't wish to receive any more books, I can return the shipping statement marked "cancel." If I don't cancel, I will receive 4 brand-new novels every month and be billed just $6.24 per book in the U.S. or $6.74 per book in Canada. That's a savings of at least 22% off the cover price. It's quite a bargain! Shipping and handling is just 50¢ per book in the U.S. and 75¢ per book in Canada.* I understand that accepting the 2 free books and gifts places me under no obligation to buy anything. I can always return a shipment and cancel at any time. Even if I never buy another book, the two free books and gifts are mine to keep forever.

194/394 MDN F4XY

Name	(PLEASE PRINT)	
Address		Apt. #
City	State/Prov.	Zip/Postal Code

Signature (if under 18, a parent or guardian must sign)

Mail to the **Harlequin® Reader Service:**
IN U.S.A.: P.O. Box 1867, Buffalo, NY 14240-1867
IN CANADA: P.O. Box 609, Fort Erie, Ontario L2A 5X3

Want to try two free books from another line?
Call 1-800-873-8635 or visit www.ReaderService.com.

* Terms and prices subject to change without notice. Prices do not include applicable taxes. Sales tax applicable in N.Y. Canadian residents will be charged applicable taxes. Offer not valid in Quebec. This offer is limited to one order per household. Not valid for current subscribers to the Romance Collection or the Romance/Suspense Collection. All orders subject to credit approval. Credit or debit balances in a customer's account(s) may be offset by any other outstanding balance owed by or to the customer. Please allow 4 to 6 weeks for delivery. Offer available while quantities last.

Your Privacy—The Harlequin® Reader Service is committed to protecting your privacy. Our Privacy Policy is available online at www.ReaderService.com or upon request from the Harlequin Reader Service.

We make a portion of our mailing list available to reputable third parties that offer products we believe may interest you. If you prefer that we not exchange your name with third parties, or if you wish to clarify or modify your communication preferences, please visit us at www.ReaderService.com/consumerschoice or write to us at Harlequin Reader Service Preference Service, P.O. Box 9062, Buffalo, NY 14269. Include your complete name and address.

ROM13R

Stay in the festive spirit next month with Rebecca Winters's
MARRY ME UNDER THE MISTLETOE, the second story
in the sparkling GINGERBREAD GIRLS trilogy!

THEIR HANDS BRUSHED, and the contact sent a warm sensation through her body. His eyes held hers for a moment before he examined the nutcracker.

"I—I love this one." Her voice faltered in reaction to his nearness. "This white uniform makes him stand out. It's an exact replica of the uniforms they wore, down to the black hat and green-and-gold trim on the cuffs and bottom of the jacket."

His husky tone set her pulse racing. "I'll take it."

"Good. I'll find the box for it in the back and wrap it for you."

She couldn't breathe until she was away from him. Good grief. She'd always heard about widow's hormones, but had never given it any thought until now.

Andrea's hands were unsteady as she wrapped the gift in green foil with a red ribbon. He gave her his credit card. She put the receipt in the sack before handing him everything.

"Mom and I appreciate your business." She flashed him a smile. "Merry Christmas. Since I'm closing up, I'll walk you to the door."

Andrea knew she was being obvious, but she wanted him to leave and never come back. It was the exact opposite of her experience with him the first time he'd come in the shop. She couldn't afford to make more of a fool of herself than she already had. He could have no idea that seeing him again had been very hard on her.

Oddly enough, she sensed he wasn't ready to go yet. If he knew she was a widow, he wouldn't be able to leave fast enough, but he hadn't asked.

A tiny nerve pulsed at the side of his hard mouth before he opened the door. "Thank you again for your generosity to my daughter. Merry Christmas." He hesitated for a moment, then left.

To her chagrin, Andrea was strongly attracted to him. His sensual appeal reached down to the deepest part of her, bringing her alive again after more than a year. She was so vulnerable right now, it was frightening. If he came near her again, intuition told her a man like him could become an addiction.

Don't miss
MARRY ME UNDER THE MISTLETOE,
available November 2013—and look out for
Casey's story, the third and final installment from the
GINGERBREAD GIRLS, in December!